John William Jones in the north east of England in 1949, from where he draws inspiration for characters and story lines. He has had a lifelong affinity with aviation and is an accomplished light aircraft pilot.

To my wife, family members and friends around the world who inspired a lot of the characters, not forgetting the Pugs, Teddy and Arthur.

John William Jones

# LATITUDE 55°02' NORTH, LONGITUDE 1°42' WEST

AUSTIN MACAULEY PUBLISHERS™

LONDON • CAMBRIDGE • NEW YORK • SHARJAH

A CIP catalogue record for this title is available from the British Library.

ISBN 9781398414402 (Paperback)
ISBN 9781398414419 (ePub e-book)

www.austinmacauley.com

First Published 2022
Austin Macauley Publishers Ltd®
1 Canada Square
Canary Wharf
London
E14 5AA

# Introduction

Go on, click the refresh button for earthly myths and mysteries, it's about time.

In this rampaging era of computer-generated science and technology, one could be forgiven to believe that there are few inexplicable things left in this terrestrial bubble or at least stuff that can mystify the mere mortal.

The supernatural is being phased out by the boffins – go against them and you are likely to be carted off by men in white coats. It appears that all we have left are repeat TV brain-bytes such as *The Twilight Zone* or *Tales of the Unexpected* to stretch our imagination, jangle the nerves or even bewilder us.

Our attention is drawn away from mother earth in favour of the extra-terrestrial universe that is so far removed from our tiny little existences that it becomes almost irrelevant, the fact that our sun will develop into a red dwarf or the milky way is spiralling into a mega black hole and will disappear or something in a squillion years' time makes no sense to us.

Give us Homo sapiens something conceivably tangible akin to witchcraft, haunted castles, the Lochness monster or bigfoot and we are hooked, to focus on our planet warts and all can excite, exhilarate, intrigue or even frighten us, this is what gives us those good to be alive days when the birds sing and the sun shines.

# Prologue
# Holocene Epoch

They lived on the high ground now that the days were much longer and much, much warmer than when their ancestors dominated the land; they still fashioned flint for their arrowheads and axes rather than the revered moulded bronze tools and weapons developed by their pugnacious neighbours. Wolves, bears and big cats roamed freely, always on the hunt for an easy meal.

This high ground in North Northumberland about 1400 feet above sea level known today as Simonside Ridge was sanctuary to Gurd and his gathering of ancient people, with uninterrupted views in every direction enabling a fortress like settlement on the escarpment.

Forays to the river and forests in the valley below were only for the strongest and fittest as their main threat was not the beasts but the lowlanders who considered them as wild quarry to be harnessed into slavery or worse.

Gurd knew it was approaching that time when the sun was at its highest, the daylight lasted the longest and the air at lower levels was almost too hot to breathe. He wasn't to know about the Mid-Holocene warm period 5000 years ago that was heating up the planet, rivers ran at a trickle and lakes dried up, this was his natural world. It was that time when he would crouch on the highest boulder and watch the small hillock in the far distance on the horizon immediately below the sun, his reason being that when only a boy, he witnessed the shaft of strange coloured light reaching towards the sun followed by the ear bursting thunderous booms that shuddered through the rocks into his body.

# Chapter 1
# Who Is Going to Believe Me?

On summer days, you will find me lying on my back on a sun lounger in my small but private sheltered garden. It faces south west so it traps and amplifies the weak northern English sunshine to that very human temperature in the mid-twenties Celsius range. I love the sunshine and that life-giving feeling of radiated heat on your face, the stuff of life, something to do with being born a Cancerian in July and believe is the reason for me suffering a bout of Seasonal Affective Disorder nearly every winter.

I was alone, Hazel had just nipped out to do a round robin of shopping that usually resulted in filling at least five bags for life so I settled into a bit of me time now that I was retired just staring up into the clear, blue sky with only a hint of cirrus as far as the eye could see, reminiscing about the heady days with my flying buddies who I never see anymore.

At this time of year, afternoons are a busy time overhead with the big, silver birds ploughing across the sky every five or ten minutes leaving their condensation trails in a quadruple, triple or twin format depending on the number of jet engines they have, hard to discern for the ordinary observer but having had a life-long affinity with aviation, I can usually guess rightly the aircraft types even though they are seven miles above the Earth's surface. Most of these aircraft travelled east to west and west to east, to and from Europe and beyond to and from North America in this dedicated UK airspace for through air traffic separated by only a thousand feet in opposing directions.

There are various live radar tracker apps for smart phones, but I never bothered much as they usually only give an airline flight number that never tells the real story behind each flight and is why I gaze in wonderment at these insular jet-propelled, winged, aluminium pods and transport my mind on board to imagine the million and one things going on inside them. This particular one I've been watching for the past few minutes from about fifty miles away is routing West and has two contrails from outboard engines, most probably a Boeing 777 with at least two hundred and fifty passengers and up to fourteen crew including two pilots. There's always a minimum of two pilots just in case one of them has a dodgy prawn for lunch, unless it's doubling as a training flight or another company pilot is repositioning via the jump seat. These days there's no call for a flight engineer who used to manage a host of systems on earlier, first-generation, multi-engine jet aircraft. Airline operators can get away with one pilot if the aircraft has only twenty seats or less, so you're stuffed if he is the one that has the out-of-date seafood unless one of the passengers has got a PPL at the very least. As things go, life in their day job as a long-haul captain or a three-ring first officer is pretty straight forward when every conceivable function on this wonder machine can be automated, key in the course, speed required and altitude for any waypoint or glide slope in the world and sit back. The hard bit for these guys is getting into those seats in the first place with years of training, examinations and flight tests that cannot be failed along with financial hardship by most that will take a very long time to pay off even for the lucky ones.

These days, looking up at the crisp blue sky exacerbates the several black floaters I have had for decades but generally I have pretty good eyesight for a guy nearing his sell by date. I only require bog-standard, off-the-shelf reading glasses for the very small print in poor light, particularly restaurant menus in that so called ambience although I can still manage a newspaper in the daylight. During my flying days, the Civil Aviation Authority appointed medical doctor recommended as a precaution for me to have some prescription varifocals for the very tiny stuff on the aviation charts and landing plates while in the cockpit mainly to compensate for the rapid alternate near to longer vision required, it was only in the last year or two I found the need to use them only occasionally when navigating, suppose it's just sign of getting old, another is taking a full forty eight hours to recover from a round of golf, mind you without a buggy.

The Boeing was making the usual rapier-like progress without deviation. Knowing the orientation of my house, I calculated on a heading of 280° with most probably a cruising ground speed of 500 mph. There were two contrails merging into one just behind the aircraft's tail clearly visible sparkling like a radiant cut diamond in the strong sunshine. I often felt the urge to wave like most people do when a ship is leaving port to a distant land as I knew full well that at least some of the window seat passengers would be staring down to the Earth on such a clear day, as their GPS screens would indicate the aircraft symbol crossing the coastline into Northern

England, something to look down at rather than the odd gas rig or ship on the grey blue formless North Sea. From 35,000 feet, it is possible to pick out a blue whale if its blowing near the surface but there's more chance of winning the lottery, overland individual big buildings can be made out but it is impossible to see a half-naked old man waving from his back garden, which is just as well. When travelling by air, I always took the A or F window seat just in front or just behind the wing so as I could see the ground and track the journey to pass the time by trying to identify in my head without a map where we were by the landmarks, such as large rivers, coast lines, mountains and airports. For these passengers, the single runway, zero seven, two five at Newcastle International Airport would be easily visible looking down on their port side. They would even see the River Tyne snaking off towards Hexham, where static steam plumes hung above the chipboard factory. If they look further afield to the west, trouble is that their necks get cricked looking out of that tiny window. It's best to get a drone if you want an aerial view and watch it on your smart device on the ground. Nowadays, these drones have revolutionised TV film making for the better.

It's a unique surreal world sitting inside an airliner while having a gin and tonic at Mach 0.84 nearer to the speed of sound than not, streaking through the heart-stopping, cold, hardly-breathable, rarefied air almost seven miles above mean sea level with the only link to the creature world being a radio wave or a radar beam. But for these, you are autonomous to the extreme – you may as well be on the space station for all the difference it makes.

In an instant, this aircraft's contrail stopped. *Not entirely unusual*, I thought. If it had passed through an invisible warmer inverted air stream so it would or should eventually resume a little further ahead. There was a big difference this time as there was no visible silver glint of an airliner, only an unnatural, faint, magenta-coloured, spherical cloud. Maybe my line of vision was behind its trajectory, so I looked further ahead, then back, then further ahead again. Nothing, not a sign. The trail just ended in a clean cut, nothing in front, below, above or behind, nothing. I took my sunglasses off and rubbed my eyes, still nothing. So I reached for my opera-sized Canon binoculars and scanned the crisp, blue sky and the now slowly expanding and dissipating artificial, white cloud, formerly the twin condensation trails. I was still not convinced that something strange had happened, as to refocus on something moving so fast at that distance with handheld binoculars is really difficult. It was probably miles off the anticipated track by now; take your eyes off an aircraft for a few seconds and its remarkably hard to get a new fix unless you can follow the contrail to the front. In this case, I could no longer do that.

I thought it must have been an optical illusion caused by a natural phenomenon, as nothing just disappears for no reason. Or was I having a senior moment? Had I dozed off, or worse, causing my mind to play tricks?

Blaming myself for becoming an old fart, I tried to dismiss the whole thing but I was still intrigued and possibly troubled as Hazel struggled through the front door with enough food shopping to survive a period of nuclear fallout.

"What's wrong, Will?" she said. "You've got your mad eyes on."

That exclusive term she uses when she detects that I'm seriously disturbed or troubled. Something to do with her being a white witch, I always thought, along with her extra sensory perception and her ability to suss people at a glance. Not that she is a practitioner of folk magic.

"You'll just think I'm daft," I said, and explained as succinctly as I could what had just happened only minutes ago over our back garden.

"Well your face hasn't drooped, and your speech isn't slurred, so if you are that troubled, why don't you give someone you know at the airport a call?"

"Good afternoon, Newcastle Tower Operations. Sandra McKay speaking. How can I help you?"

"Sandra, my name is Will, Will Surtees. I am a one-time private pilot and have had a long association with the Northumberland Aero Club. I assure you this is not a prank, my wife next to me can vouch for that. I would like to report a possible incident involving a jet airliner passing over my house in Dinnington as you possibly know is only a kilometre from yourself in the tower and is why I called you direct."

"Yes, Mr Surtees, I've got that. Can you tell me what might this incident be? But firstly, I must take some personal details, full name, address, contact numbers etc., as you know these calls are recorded and documented as a requirement by the Civil Aviation Authority."

After completing the formalities, I slowly explained in detail what I had apparently witnessed less than thirty minutes ago.

"Can I call you Will?" asked Sandra.

"Of course," I said.

"You do know that we are not usually the air traffic control service for the high level through traffic that does not affect our terminal control area and surrounding airways but I can tell you that we at Newcastle have not been advised of an incident or problems with any aircraft entering or above our airspace. I shall immediately pass your concerns on to our senior controller, and he will no doubt call you back if need be, but I'm fairly certain your observations are due to the atmospheric conditions, probably the beautiful sunshine we are having today." On that, she abruptly and quite formally said, "I must go. Goodbye, Mr Surtees," and disconnected, clearly not wanting to be drawn into any further conversation about my observations.

Miss Mackay obviously had more important things to do rather than humour an old codger like me calling out of the blue with such imaginings, which was fair enough, I suppose, thinking it was the end of the matter and I could now dissolve back into obscurity.

In less than fifteen minutes, the house phone rang. Caller withheld no number. I would normally never answer because of the infernal PPI and thieving scammers. I hated cold calling with vengeance, but intuitively I did pick up this time.

"Hello, is that Will? Will Surtees?"

"Yes, it is," I replied.

"My name is Dan Parkinson, senior air traffic controller at Newcastle airport. I've just listened to a recording of the telephone conversation you've had with my colleague, Sandra, within the last half an hour here at air traffic control regarding your concerns about a possible incident in the sky overhead your house in Dinnington. We really do appreciate your call but I can only reiterate that we do not have any information to substantiate a problem with any aircraft in the skies in and around our airspace. Will, I'm going off duty in about fifteen minutes, and will be passing through Dinnington on my way home. Can I drop by your house to get you to endorse a transcript copy of your apparent sighting for our records? You know what the Civil Aviation Authority are like; you never know but an aircraft may have had a temporary fault of some kind that has not been reported. By the way, will your wife be there? It will only take a few minutes."

"Yes, I suppose that's okay. We're not planning to go anywhere soon today," I replied.

"That's fine. I'll see you both in about an hour. Oh and by the way, can I ask that you keep this to yourself and not to speak to anyone at least until after our meeting?"

"Okay, I didn't intend to, as I already feel like a right wolly," I told him.

He told me not to worry as they are not permitted to divulge anything. I thought that was a bit of a relief, half expecting a visit from the men in white coats.

"Who was that?" Hazel asked.

"Some air traffic controller guy from the airport wants to call in and see us about what I saw, something to do with his paperwork for the CAA. He'll be here in an hour. I wish I'd never called now; I'm starting to feel like a twenty-four carat wanker."

"Never mind, he'll probably think you're a village-ite instead like I do, so you better put some clothes on and cover up your bits," she said.

'Village-ite' was her not-so-endearing, made-up word for a village idiot type, or should I say, intellectually challenged. *Not such a bad existence*, I think, as they can get away with that 'ignorance is bliss' approach to life. For the rest of us, a little knowledge causes us to think too deeply, which can be bad for blood pressure. I know I wasn't a townie like Hazel and maybe I was a village-ite and just didn't know it yet, but I do know that I'm often criticised for blurting stuff out without too much thought. A Surtees's trait, I'm led to believe.

# Chapter 2
# A Routine Departure

It was a beautiful morning at Frankfurt Hahn airport as it should have been on this summer solstice morning, 20th June 2020. Having arrived two hours earlier from Milwaukee, USA, flight number November Alpha 426 with her call sign 'Fire-crest 426', a Boeing triple seven belonging to the United States airline 'Northern Arc Air' was in the final preparation stages for the eight-hour return trip. On a day like today in the northern hemisphere, there were no adverse en-route weather considerations so the planned track would be as normal. North west on a heading of three one zero direct towards the UK on a cleared flight level of three six zero, overhead EGNT (Newcastle Airport) in north-east England then a left turn West towards EGPK (Prestwick Airport) on the western coast of mainland Scotland, coasting out towards Rockall north west of Ireland crossing the Atlantic South of Iceland, then Greenland, over the North American Great Lakes and then home – some four thousand miles away well within maximum range.

On stand, hooked up to the many ground support systems, Fire-crest 426 was gleaming after a recent three-thousand-hour nose to tail overhaul in her mainly olive green and white livery with a silver polished alloy under belly proudly sporting for virtually the whole length of her fuselage 'NorthernarcAir.Com' in huge verdana font in the same olive green. Her distinction was the black, orange and red flashes simulating a bird's crest over the flight deck section.

For this trip, there would be only two flight deck crew, Captain Jeff Clark, a fifty-six-year-old Canadian. A veteran of flying with fifteen thousand hours logged as pilot in command, starting with Twin Otter floatplanes, and his first command at twenty-two had a lot of hands-on flying experience to draw from. But after all this time, he did not really miss it in his private life and would rather be somewhere with his Belarusian wife and teenage daughters, Anna and Josie, than recreational flying when at home. There was more than enough time spent in air on his day job that was mostly routine 'flying on rails' now, but it gave them all a great life and he was a very happy man with retirement just over the horizon at sixty, when the golf course would beckon with Lada, who certainly lived up to her name sake. The Slavic Goddess of love and beauty even now at fifty-two loved to play a round of golf when they had the very occasional chance. Her Russian expletives were a joy to behold if a putt was missed.

Jeff had become tired of living out of his chocolate brown, soft, leather travel bag in a hotel room like the night before. The glamour had long since waned, and once the four-ringed uniform jacket was hung in the wardrobe, he became just another anonymous guest passing through unnoticed, not that he was bothered.

On the other hand, the relative, rooky first officer, twenty-five-year-old Steve Baumgartner loved the post flight get together at the hotel with the cabin crew. Steve was no Chippendale, but the uniform disguised this young boy of a pilot into a Leonardo DiCaprio look alike, so it was worn every minute he was in the public gaze. Steve had spent most of his childhood ensconced in his bedroom on flight simulators and swatting up on anything and everything to do with aviation. He would eventually breeze through every flight handling test and exam. Going that fast tracked him onto the big jets, although he would still have to put in another two million air miles or five thousand hours to become captain one day. Still way off in about five years from now, in the 1940s, he already would have been a veteran skipper on a B-17 Flying Fortress by now or maybe a Fock-Wulfe Condor, given his ancestry.

A complement of twelve cabin crew split more or less evenly across the genders. They were a well-seasoned group and would undoubtedly be able to handle every known situation that may arise. Once on board, they harmonised and clicked into gear, putting any personal issues they may have had out of mind with their infectious, confident, bubbly enthusiasm that immediately transferred to the 281 passengers as they happily stowed their hand baggage into the overhead lockers and settled into their seats, a result of loving what they do and the thought of being home back in the States soon.

The 295 souls on board didn't fill the aircraft but they were more than enough to make the flight very viable compared to the early months of 2020, when the aviation industry was virtually closed down due to the Coronavirus pandemic. It had only been a few weeks since an anti-viral injection had been developed and deemed approved for general use, therefore, it had become mandatory for anyone stepping onto an aircraft to produce a uniquely QR coded certificate of vaccination against COVID-19 along with their passports. If this document did not scan, you did not fly, no exceptions. These passengers, as always, would make the trip eventful if not interesting. Their very existence and influence on others could easily affect another ten thousand human beings on the ground across the world. Even without the professional basketball team on board with countless social media followers, multiply that up by the number of aircrafts in the sky in any one day and the numbers are staggering. That is the magnitude of Earth's aviation travel industry. Unusually, there were no infants or juveniles on this route today, probably due to most being tied up with school exams given the time of year. This would give the cabin crew some breathing space for a refreshing change. There were two dogs, however, travelling in business class with Mrs Mary Larssen, who called them Teddy and Arthur. Two black Pugs who would have been better named Reggie and Ronald, the infamous gangsters, although they weren't natural brothers. Arthur came along a year later when he was rescued from a family that couldn't or wouldn't give him the love he rightly deserved. Both quickly became seasoned flyers in their separate life supporting travel pods; they never left Mary's side. Well-fed and exercised beforehand, they would hunker down and snore like drunken sailors in an almost catatonic state for hours. Let them out and they would mug everything in sight. That's after eating anything that even looked or smelled like food but nothing was off the table as far as the terrible twins were concerned. They still had the capacity to melt your heart with one, googly-eyed glance.

Mary Larssen adored her Pugs, they went everywhere with her. They were her companions, even more so since her granddaughter recently left home for university only as far as the next state but still too far away for that irreplaceable human contact. She had brought her up from that beautiful, innocent age of four when both of her parents were tragically killed in a skiing accident while visiting their ancestral home in Norway.

Mary had been staying in Germany for the past six months to be with her ageing and infirm Norwegian brother who had settled there after the Second World War. After such a long and arduous time, she and her dogs were all looking forward to getting back to a normal life in the wide-open, green spaces of Muskego, Wisconsin.

Everyone seated, safety belts fastened, and the final 'paperwork' done as every flight complement is told, the giant thunderbird slowly pushed back. Jeff and Steve cycled the starters in sequence to wind up the two, massive GE 90 jets so that when in position and the tug unhitched, they were ready to go with the engines up to temperature and rumbling at about twenty-four percent of their power. Thumbs up from the ground engineer after unplugging his flight deck com feed, leaving the fourteen wheels as the only physical contact with terra firma. With the mighty jet engines spooled up to forty percent, Fire-crest 426 heaved forward to taxi speed on her way to runway zero three, lined up and cleared for take-off. Jeff pushed the throttles up to eighty-five percent of maximum power, smoothing out the engine rumble to a thunderous roar.

Steve transmitted, "Rolling zero three."

Within fifteen seconds, Jeff firmly pulled back on the yoke and this magnificent machine took the weight of 250 tonnes on her wings causing them to gently flex upwards, then almost defying the laws of physics majestically rose nose up into the sky, tucked all fourteen wheels into her under belly and slowly banked at fifteen degrees to the left thrusting into the clear, blue yonder like a flashing blade in the morning sunshine as she turned north westwards heading towards the German west coast to cross four hundred miles of North Sea before next landfall.

# Chapter 3
# Delta Five One Zero

Dr Isaac Penfold MBE, or I.P. to only a few in his circle or league during his Cambridge days studying a master's degree in the Faculty of Science and Engineering, a very serious thinker and delved into almost every discipline of physics to satisfy his insatiable curiosity of things beyond explanation or so they may have appeared to mere mortals. I.P. was not officially attached to the RAF or any of the other of the British armed forces, but he was highly paid as a civil servant. Very few were above his station in terms of influence and authority in the United Kingdom's command hierarchy, so much so as to having a seat at the government's COBR meetings when required and usually only dressed informally but stylishly wearing a Ralph Lauren polo shirt, stone-coloured Chinos and green suede Wallabees that set him apart from the men in suits.

I.P.'s job was to head up at the last count a team of forty-nine specially selected personnel made up of so-called but appropriately named misfits and weirdos, unofficially known as the M and W squad. Most of them could give Albert Einstein, Carl Sagan, Professor Brian Cox or Arthur C Clark a run for their money but as sure as hell not as TV show presenters because of the risk of frightening the kids to death.

The official name of this wing of the UK Gov's MI5 was the Department for Scientific Determination of Unexplained Phenomenon. These guys and gals or whatever gender some of them may have related to were mainly residential inmates but certainly not confined to Barracks similar to the civilian status for those at Bletchley Park during Turin's Enigma code breaker days. Most were fully boarded in sumptuous rooms at Gilsland Hall so that they were in the main freed from domesticity, formerly a convalescing home for shell shocked soldiers during the great war. Very fitting, given the disposition of some of these DSDUP members drawn from an assortment of UK residents, not necessarily British citizens. All were free to come and go as they chose and were never required to check in or out as it were. They decided themselves how they worked or went about their processes unless I.P. summoned them for a briefing on a particular matter. They were detailed to investigate not necessarily in their own field of expertise, such as their brain power. Some were positively nocturnal, some would stay awake for days on end and some you didn't see for a week or two. Most were loners and hardly the sociable animals we are led to believe that humans are. Some even seemed perfectly normal but just too bright to fit in unless they pretended to be ordinary. Four of them would regularly clean up at the Greenhead Arms pub quiz; the one thing they had in common was that whatever mystery matter they were presented with, they would have a plausible theory on it or at least plausible to the not so many people like I.P.

Sitting at his desk in his office at the MoD's unworldly research centre at Spadeadam situated deep inside a remote area of West Northumberland abutting the Scottish Border known as Delta five one zero rumoured to be the UK equivalent of Area 51 in the States, the ID numbering similarity is probably no coincidence.

I.P. slid the RAF embossed, maroon, calf-skin, square-sided briefcase towards him, dialled in the code, pinged the brass catches and slowly opened the lid to reveal a single blue wallet folder tied with a red ribbon and sealed with a red wax HM Gov stamp. Earlier that day, he had been formally advised by GCHQ to expect a hand delivery from a secure Royal Air Force detachment.

The folder was rubber block stamped that was probably manufactured in 1942. 'CLASSIFIED HD' in the usual three-eighths of an inch, high, red capital letters not seriously thought to mean 'HUNG if DIVULGED'. Very few knew just how close to the truth that really was. Hanging is still legal in Britain for treason; it was really boffin code for 'high discretion' rather than 'top secret'. The only category above this level was usually reserved for spies and war strategies. Handwritten in capitals underneath in blue ink undoubtedly by a square nibbed Parker fountain pen was the underlined sub-title, 'THE ABORA EFFECT'. This folder contained only one four page Ministry of Defence headed document, probably typed up by a mechanical Remington Rand model 5 as these reports never even got close to a typewriter that was plugged into an electricity supply, let alone Microsoft Word and iCloud. These documents always looked and smelled like they had been archeologically unearthed from Churchill's war rooms; mind you, they could easily have been secretly archived for decades as some of these documents were not let out into the public arena until someone decided how it was to be redacted, not this one though the paper was new.

This summary of 'THE ABORA EFFECT' papers read:

*On 21st June 2018 in CAVOK weather conditions, two RAF Typhoon FGR4 all-weather jet fighter bombers fully armed of 1435 Squadron (recently returned from the Falkland Islands) took off from RAF Leuchars at 11:45 am, detailed to join a NATO training exercise over the north of England extending out over the North Sea into Delta five one three a designated Danger Area of Intense Aerial Activity. 'Blue leader' piloted by Flight Lieutenant Jack Naylor and 'Blue Wing' piloted by Flight Sergeant Leonard Williams entered Delta five one three at 11:59 am with instructions to seek out a F35 lightening 11 (raptor) of the USAF for simulated destruction. Blue wing was first to engage the F35 with Blue Leader in pursuit. Heading west at Mach.1.24, flight level three five zero (35,000 feet), QNH 1013.2 Blue Wing was observed to enter into a faint magenta coloured orb and 'disappear', all efforts by Blue Leader to raise Blue Wing on the specific operational radio frequency failed. Suspecting radio failure, Blue Leader alerted Newcastle Radar to keep a listen out on their frequencies. They responded to say they had not identified any unknown transponder squawks on their radar scopes. Blue Leader returned to Leuchars and a major Search and Rescue operation was put in place. At 13:05 pm, the aircraft was declared lost in action over the North Sea. For national security reasons, the incident was not put into the public domain, the last known radar trace provided by RAF Boulmer was Longitude 01°42' West, Latitude 55°02'*

North, approximately 0.7 nautical miles North East of EGNT, Newcastle International Airport.

On 24th June 2018, the wreckage of a military aircraft was discovered in a remote mountainous area on the Canary Island of La Palma along with the severely injured pilot close-by, still wearing his parachute harness by a lone goat farmer who had witnessed its descent for only a few seconds before hitting the ground. The evidence indicates that the pilot had ejected only seconds before impact. The pilot sustained fractures to both femurs, multiple superficial contusions and lacerations, and although there were no significant head injuries, he was in a bewildered and stressed state. After two days of diplomatic wrangling between British and Spanish authorities, the pilot was airlifted back to the UK for further treatment and the wreckage crated up for shipping and subsequent forensic inspection having been securely guarded by Spanish Special Forces during that time.

The pilot and wreckage was that of the missing British pilot Flight Sergeant Williams and the RAF Typhoon FRG4 of 1435 Squadron.

The formal explanation put forward by the UK government for the incident was that the aircraft damaged the intake nozzle during an air-to-air refuelling rendezvous over the Atlantic returning from the Faulkland Islands and simply ran out of fuel. The pilot had used the remaining fuel to head for the nearest airfield managed to glide for the last of the 100 miles to the nearest land being the Spanish Canary island of La Palma.

A transcript of the witness's account leading up to locating the aircraft and its pilot was vague and only his repeated quote of "La Abora" that relates to the name of a *mythical sun goddess from the time of the Guanches period made any sense that the aircraft must have appeared out of the sun's glare. He later managed to describe it as being a magenta colour at the time and not the usual colour of the sun's brilliant yellow gold.*

*Flight Sergeant Leonard Williams was first interviewed on 26th June 2018 and subsequently on four other occasions by the RAF's own internal air accident investigation unit. He was deemed too unfit at the time to be interviewed by the Spanish authorities prior to this. On each occasion, Sergeant Williams's statement never wavered in so much that he recalls being in pursuit of the F35 climbing steeply with after burner power through 35,000 feet when he entered a strange purple hue. The engines and every other system on the aircraft immediately closed down. There was no feeling of any G forces, neither negative nor positive, just a sense of being stationary almost floating in serene quiet. The aircraft was totally dead, he did press the transmit button and tried to radio a mayday call, but all that he could hear was his own throbbing pulse in his ears. He was certain that this state of suspension only lasted two minutes when suddenly the purple hue cleared and the vision of the earth came hurtling into view. At that point, he pulled the ejector seat release handle; there was no accounting for the lost four days in his mind, not even a minute.*

*Since the incident, Flight Sergeant Williams is stood down from his pilot duties pending the outcome of ongoing investigations.*

*I believe that's over to us, the M and W's are going to love this one*, I.P. thought as he pondered how to brief this one out.

In the end, he decided that each individual member of the team was to be invited by strict appointment into a guarded room and left alone with the file to read for thirty minutes and record their initial thoughts, theories or whatever they had, in no more than a hundred words. All in all, the whole process took about thirty-six hours. Depending on what I.P. read as they each left the room, he detailed the now fifty M&W's into three compatible groups in various numbers to follow up alternative avenues of investigation. He had had to narrow down these theoretical responses because as expected, they were all different. Some were totally off the wall, but most not entirely poles apart. The obvious three lines of enquiry were based on:

Firstly…the supernatural, such as psychic powers, mythical monsters, ghouls and ghosts etc.

Secondly…extra-terrestrial, such as solar activity, black holes and UFOs, etc.

And thirdly…known Earthly phenomena, such as the weather, seismic activity, gravity and solar activity etc.

Potentially, they had an almost infinitesimal amount of subject matter that would have to be filtered out for practicality, thinking all of these subjects are blurred at the edges somewhat without absolute scientific resolution as even gravity is unfathomable as a state. Einstein himself described it as a consequence of mass. *What in hell is a consequence in this context? That's a coverall statement, if ever there was one,* he thought.

This particular written response intrigued I.P. more than most and read as follows…

*Latitude 55° 02' North, Longitude 01° 42 West pinpoints the centre of an area of high ground in the north-east of England, known as Toft Hill. It is approx. 300 feet above mean sea level. As far as I have determined, it is the confluence of a multitude of the Earth's ley lines or black streams, thought to be only relatively weak energy forces of an unknown origin or state. My theory is at this exact grid point, this location forms a 'portal' for these earthly energy forces, I will call them 'mother nature particles' for the time being.*

I.P. wanted to give her the opportunity to substantiate this theory on the ground so the youthful, seemingly peerless Mia Gaustaad was chosen to lead team three, accompanied by ten other hand-picked members of the M and W's.

Mia Gaustaad's persona could be summed up as being a psychic new ager having ditched studying astrophysics at the University of Massachusetts and moving to the Orkney Islands to pursue a hippy-type lifestyle, earning a subsistence existence by assisting on archaeological surveys around ancient monuments, particularly standing stones. Mia was by no means on the breadline, and money wasn't important to her in terms of extravagant possessions so long as she could afford to subsidise her travel to wherever her obsessive curiosity enticed her. Since the age of seven, Mia had spent every possible moment of the sixteen years since exploring if there was science-based evidence behind these mysterious energies and the ancient and modern myths surrounding these amazing structures. Although nothing published, she had documented a mountain of stuff on the subject, her charting of these forces such as ley lines, arawn pathways or black streams all referring to similar Earthly phenomena led her to that exact same spot at Toft Hill over which the Typhoon FRG4 vanished at 35,000 feet on 21st June 2018.

Two months earlier, while drinking a pint of Tenants lager alone at Captain Flints bar in Kirkwall, Mia had been approached by a striking, slightly greying, forty-something guy who was obviously on the same wavelength, or as she deduced by the amount of knowledge he had, on the subject of standing stone structures that was certainly not gained by reading *The Complete Idiots Guide to Paganism*. So far in her young life, it was a very unusual experience for her to meet someone like him, not that she mixed informally with many people. They talked nonstop for hours about this seemingly common mythical interest when nearing the time they had to go their separate ways for the night, he casually invited her to visit Castlerigg with him in the Cumbrian Lake District. Coincidentally, these ancient standing stones were only a taxi ride from Delta Five One Zero. He had visited this mysterious site many times with his parents as an only child. Thinking it was a genuinely innocent gesture and feeling relaxed in this stranger's company, Mia was minded that she would very much like to do that sometime especially in the company of this man that intrigued her so much. Finally someone she could talk to with a comfortable ease as well as thinking he was so handsome, something that had never crossed her mind in the company of other undistinguished men.

The following evening while finishing her third half pint of cold lager sitting alone with her natural beautiful poise on a bar stool courteously resisting the offers of the local chancers to buy her a drink, she received this text message:

*A car will pick you up at 0800 in the morning to take you to Kirkwall airport. I thought you might like to see those stones we talked about last night, I've spoken to your boss who is an old friend of mine. He has kindly released you from your surveying duties for a day or two…bring a toothbrush.*

*Regards, I.P.*


The only other text she had had that day was from the one person she cared for very deeply, her gran who wanted to tell her that she was travelling back to the USA soon. Lots of good news in the same day. Not that she ever got outwardly excited, she was intrigued by this man's invitation and felt she could do with a break from being battered by the wind and sleet on that exposed Orkney hillside, not that it affected her physically very much being from hardy Norwegian stock.

Mia, with her natural, outdoor, tanned complexion, was a stunning specimen of health and vigour, the type of young woman that could easily get away with wearing a black bin liner to a red carpet affair As the blue RAF Free Lander driven by a young WRAF corporal wearing grey-blue camouflage fatigues arrived at the lodge at precisely 7:59 am. Without striking up a conversation, the driver drove her directly to the Kirkwall airport. 'Control' marked by a big black C on a yellow background above the door at the foot of the control tower building. Only yards away on the tarmac apron, the twin-engine, grey-blue, unmarked Beach Baron stood ready with its navigation lights on and strobes flashing. Another young, identical-looking WRAF private was standing at the foot of the aircraft steps.

"Miss Gaustaad, security has been taken care of. This is your aircraft; you can sit up front with the pilot. Is there anything you require?" she asked politely but spoke as an instruction.

Mia said, "No, thank you, everything is fine," as she stepped into the cabin placing her multi-coloured canvas Coach Rivington backpack onto one of the seats behind the crews as she slid her lithe and shapely body onto the right-hand front co-pilots seat.

"Good morning, Mia, I'm so glad you decided to come," came from a voice she instantly recognised from the captain's seat next to her.

# Chapter 4
# At the Queen's Pleasure

"I.P., Charles here. We have a live incident involving an American airliner over the UK. We think it could be connected to this Abora business; a helicopter is ready to take you to Newcastle International Airport. The flight will take about twenty minutes. I'm already here with our people, you will be fully briefed on arrival."

Isaac whispered something into Mia's ear. She did not answer but quickly collected her coat, and they were soon on their way to the rooftop heliport. Waiting for them, rotors turning and ready to lift, was a green, white and yellow Dauphin AS 365. The two crew wearing red jump suits, to the untrained eye a Great North Air Ambulance, yes designed to attract attention but for the wrong reasons in this case such as the need to maintain the anonymity of the real passengers and crew and their purpose.

Within twenty minutes, the Dauphin landed on the general aviation South apron at Newcastle airport where a red Land Rover, eight-seat fire tender, driven by an undoubtedly armed 'fire fighter' most certainly detailed from a discrete British Regiment, was ready to ferry them to the airport control tower via the internal perimeter track, avoiding the need to pass through any airport airside security checks. The Great North Air Ambulance immediately lifted off and headed West back to a shed at Albemarle barracks to be locked away out of sight until a new assignment with possibly a new livery was called for.

The driver keyed in the tower door code. I.P. and Mia followed as he showed them into an office marked 'Senior Air Traffic Controller'.

"Good to see you, I.P.," said Charles, holding out his hand. "This must be Mia."

"Yes, nice to see you, Charles. This is Mia Gaustaad who's leading a section of my Abora team," said I.P.

"There's no time to waste, so I'll ask Dan here to fill you in on today's events. Oh and this is Brad Shoultts who's representing our partners across the pond. He's aware of the code HD status. Over to you, Dan," said Charles.

Chief Air Traffic Controller Dan Parkinson went on to explain that an American Boeing 777 en route to Milwaukee from Frankfurt with the call sign Fire-crest 426 carrying 295 passengers and crew instantly disappeared off all radar scopes exactly one hour 37 minutes ago.

Turning the back of his hand to look at his impressive wristwatch, he said, "Its last known position was overhead longitude one degree forty-two seconds west, latitude fifty-five degrees zero two seconds north, barely five hundred yards from where we are sitting. The last radio contact was thirty minutes prior on handover from Scottish Information. There has been no pan or mayday call since; there are no reports of wreckage anywhere and the only so-called witness of anything unusual is a chap called Will Surtees who lives about a mile away in Dinnington Village." He switched on a recording of the telephone conversation with Sandra McKay. Mia and I.P listened attentively the rest of the group had already heard it at least three times before Mia and I.P. had arrived. As soon as the recording clicked off, Dan advised that he had arranged to meet this Mr Surtees at his home in less than thirty minutes from now.

Charles began to speak. "We currently have no idea what has happened to Fire-crest 426 along with the 295 people on board. In about three and a half hours from now they will be officially overdue and we cannot simply announce that it just vanished in a puff of purple smoke over Northern England under the same circumstances as an RAF jet fighter exactly two years ago to the day in 2018. Until we know more we will have to keep the lid on it, otherwise the world's aviation industry will collapse indefinitely if a story gets out that commercial aircraft are being zapped out of the skies. Let's get over to see this Will Surtees and his wife and plug that hole for now."


Nearing the time for my visitors to arrive, feeling very uncomfortable, I looked out of my front window to see a grey Mercedes people carrier with darkened windows parked across the road outside number fourteen and just then another identical MPV drew up across my drive entrance. The driver dressed like a member of an American SWAT team rang the doorbell.

I said to Hazel, "This must be them," with that apprehensive butterfly gut feeling. *Hello*, I thought, *this is not just a casual drive by visit*. I never did like the establishment as I always thought they were a threat to freedom.

"You better go and see. I'll put the kettle on," Hazel said.

"Good day," the military styled man said. "Mr Will Surtees?" he asked.

"Yes," I said. He immediately turned and nodded towards the darkened windows of the second Mercedes. Dan Parkinson quickly emerged and approached followed by another two men accompanied by a very attractive, young, blond woman.

"Good afternoon. I'm Dan. You are Will, I presume?" he didn't need to ask as he'd already seen the grey-haired guy that looked like an old sixties Californian surfer on the photo attached in my CAA file. "May we come in?"

"Yes, come in," I said as I showed them into the living room, thinking I didn't expect this kind of attention as I offered them to take a seat. Luckily, we did have room to seat six or seven at a push, not including the dining table seating in our open plan living space. Hazel popped her head around the door and asked if anyone would like tea or coffee. They all declined politely, presumably so they could get on with the urgent business at hand. Dan introduced himself to Hazel and asked if she would stay in the room.

"We'll try not to keep you too long. Will, Hazel, this is Charles. He's here on behalf of our government and has something to say to you both."

"Try not to be alarmed," Charles said, looking straight at us. "There is the possibility of some substance to what you witnessed with that high-flying aircraft over your house today. Before I can give you more detail, I must ask you both to sign these," he said as he handed us both a very official looking HM government document, sub-headed the 'Official Secrets Act', pre-printed with our full names on them. "I have to say to you both that if you decline, that is quite within your rights and it will leave me no alternative other than to place you under house arrest with immediate effect and the people in that vehicle across the road will ensure this is enforced. In the meantime, your landline, mobile phones and broadband have already been suspended."

I looked at Hazel and told her that I didn't feel like a wanker anymore, more like a criminal now and thought if it meant our freedom was at stake. It was a small price to pay to sign on the dotted line and find out what the hell was going on. It sounded like something big was kicking off and I didn't like how we had been sucked in. I looked Charles straight in the eye and told him that I wanted to see the credentials of everyone in my living room right now before I do anything. Charles reached into his pocket and opened a small, black, leather wallet to display a very shiny official silver badge in the shape of a portcullis and a warrant card bearing the name Charles Whitworth Stanley, MBE, HM Gov. Home Office. The signature below looked very like *ElizabethR*. With that, I had seen enough and didn't bother looking at the others. I looked at Hazel and noticed that look of dread on her face, fearing I was going to eject these people. I took the documents to the dining table where we both promptly signed them using Charles's black and gold roller-point Mont Blanc pen; at the same time detecting my hand starting to tremble slightly probably due to the proximity of some of the highest authority in the land.

"Now that you both have kindly done your duty as citizens, I can say that our people outside are already stood down," said Charles when I noticed the first grey Mercedes MPV moving away and slowly disappearing up the street. "Okay, Will, Hazel," Charles said. "This is what we've got and is why we had to be rather strict with you. The aircraft you saw disappear overhead this location is an American airliner that has gone missing without a trace, and for the moment, there is absolutely no explanation as to why. There was no radio contact and there are no reports of any wreckage anywhere, so it's difficult to think that the cause is terrorism. Which is bad enough, but for it to fall off the radar similar to the Malaysian MH370 incident is unthinkable and will without doubt send shock waves throughout the world's travelling public and potentially destroy the aviation industry so soon after the terrible consequences of the Covid-19 pandemic. In about four hours from now, this aircraft will be overdue at Milwaukee. There are 295 passengers and crew whose families will be waiting, so we are pretty desperate to find a plausible cause unless it turns up very soon. The reason why we've acted so quickly is to try to quell any rumours of unnatural phenomena such as extra-terrestrial activity. I will tell you that there was a similar occurrence with one of our military aircrafts, two years ago to the day, in this very same location, investigations are still ongoing although, fortunately, the aircraft and pilot were recovered some time afterwards. That's all I can disclose regarding this incident for the time being as it still remains a possible risk to national security. So Will, we want you to tell us about every last detail of what you saw."

"Well, I don't think I've got anything to add other than what I've already told that young lady at the airport."

"Are you sure?" Charles asked. "Did you see any other aircraft or objects, for instance?"

"Do you mean UFOs?"

"I mean anything at all."

"Like I said, only a very pale pink-purple coloured orb where the aircraft should have been, but I had sunglasses on and put that down to the refraction of the bright sunlight."

"Can I see your sunglasses, Will?" he said.

"Yes, here they are."

"Ah, these are good. Carreras, I see. Do you ski? Because these are excellent lenses."

"Yes, I know they are, but I've never done any skiing as such. Just a day trip to the Italian Alps just to see what it's like up there. Bloody cold, I remember, because we were not dressed for it so I, if not the whole eight of us, was glad to get back down again, but these Carreras did come in handy, not bad for eleven quid off of e-bay."

"Okay Will, I've got the model number so I'll have them checked out so we can eliminate this magenta orb thing," said Charles. "I will give you a contact number. Please call it anytime if you think of anything at all, anything."

Charles turned to Dan, I.P., Mia and Brad Shoultts individually to ask if they wished to ask any questions. The consensus was that they would almost certainly wish to talk to me further down the line, but not at the moment.

"Thank you, Hazel, Will. Dan here will keep you informed as necessary. Goodbye, for now," Charles said kindly as they got up to leave. Mia discreetly handed Hazel her card in that woman-to-woman way and reassured her. They all left as quickly as they came.

While standing at my door watching the MPV disappear to the top of the street, Mick, my neighbour, shot out of his front door and said, "Hey Will, those guys looked very official, is everything okay?"

Jokingly, I told him it was just the men in black so he would go away confused, never believing it was the actual truth. I would often do this to busybodies and wise crackers to throw them off the scent; let the Chinese whispers take over and sit back. I love it because I hate being quizzed.

"Well, Hazel that was a turn up for the books. I feel sick to my stomach, thinking about that aeroplane and all of those poor people in it."

"It's awful. Let's hope there's a simple explanation and it turns up safe. Time for a drink, I think there's nothing much we can do about it other than lie low and keep our mouths shut. If it doesn't turn up, we'll know in a few hours, I suppose," replied Hazel. Fortunately, the human condition is such that although you feel pity unless you are directly affected by tragedy, the feeling you get usually is 'I'm glad it's not me on that plane'.

"I need to get back to London," Charles announced as soon as the car started to move. "My plane is already waiting at the airport, got a meeting with the PM at the American embassy in two hours so we can sort out a statement for release when things go haywire at Milwaukee at about five o'clock this afternoon. Just so as we concur, if nothing crops up by then, it's going to have to be that flight NA 426 has disappeared over the Atlantic beyond Rockall, it's last known radar trace. Totally untrue, of course, but we cannot say that it disappeared in a puff of purple smoke over Northern England. It's bad enough if it has crashed without that. The car will take you back to five one zero directly, Brad. Dan and I will be getting out at the airport. Have a think about it on the way back and get back to me this afternoon with proposals for a line of enquiry."

"What do you think, Mia?" I.P. said, once alone sitting opposite to each other in the back of the MPV. Mia answered while looking at an Ordnance Survey app on her phone.

"First, I want to get a team on this area called 'Toft Hill' to carry out some ground radar surveillance without drawing too much attention around Will and Hazel as I noticed there were a lot of curtains twitching when we arrived. I see there's an underground gas pipeline that runs along the north side of it. Maybe I can get a couple of gas company trucks and a mile of their 'Warning. Keep out' tape and move our equipment up there."

"All of that will be ready for you at 0600 hours tomorrow," I.P. answered, very business-like. He was now very much in work mode, a very different animal.

"Hello Charles, I.P. here. We are starting with a GRS survey. I've got it set up. Our men will be on site in an hour and Mia's team will move in at first light."

"That's good, nothing to report yet at this end. We've already got the AWACS up there trawling around. Unless something crops up, an announcement will be made at seventeen thirty along the lines we talked about. May their Gods have mercy on their souls," Charles replied.

# Chapter 5
# Castlerigg

"You are a very surprising man," Mia said. "Is this yours?"

"You could say that," I.P. replied. "Maybe, just to put you at ease and to assure you I'm not trying to abduct you, it does belong to the UK Government Department that pays my salary, and a lot of British security forces know exactly where this aircraft is and who's in it. We'll be flying nonstop to Carlisle Airport overhead Inverness. Then because we are in no particular hurry, we'll take the scenic route following the Scottish rift Valley to Oban and South, skirting the Scottish west coast to Prestwick, then overland to Dumfries, then on to Carlisle. Since it's a beautiful day, I can point out the landmarks as we go if you wish."

"Yes, that would be very interesting as I've never visited these parts before, and so far, I love being here," she replied. "And who's to say that I wouldn't mind being abducted by you."

I.P. felt a slight twinge in his loins with that reply. He wasn't expecting it. Together with the faint smell of her Dolce and Gabbana light blue, his nostrils flared slightly as he reached for the trim wheel to refocus his mind on flying the Baron. Something she hadn't bothered wearing two nights before, not expecting an encounter in the pub relaxing after a windswept cold day at the standing stones of Stenness. He knew he shouldn't, but he felt unusually attracted to her. Not that any red-blooded male wouldn't be to this beautiful American girl, young enough to be his daughter.

The weather forecast was very good for the trip and for the following days ahead as they banked slightly to the right overhead Inverness to track the Caledonian Canal and Loch Ness towards Oban. He trimmed out the Baron at an altitude of 5500 feet at an airspeed of 180 knots switched on the autopilot and relaxed. All he needed to do now if necessary was turn the heading bug on the direction indicator for any minor track adjustments leaving him free to talk and point out the landmarks to Mia knowing that they were nine hundred feet above the highest point on route this being the Scottish mountain Ben Nevis.

"That large lake below and heading off into the distance ahead is Loch Ness" he said.

"Ah yes, home of the famous Nessy," she replied. "We all know about Nessy back home. It was apparently last sighted only two months ago by a young boy on his video camera by chance, but again its existence still cannot be proven."

"Well I'm not so sure about that," he whispered a reply under his breath, quickly pretending to be distracted by twiddling with the DI bug. Mia slowly turned to look at I.P. and raised her eyebrows. "There's some coffee in the bag behind my seat, if you'd like some," he said.

"I'm really a tea person," she replied. "Coffee's fine only because tea doesn't travel well in a flask."

"Could be something else we agree on, as I love tea myself," he said. "I have at least five cups a day, but it's got

47

to be my own made from Yorkshire Gold tea bags when I'm not at home where Greta makes it with the special loose stuff she buys."

"Greta," she said. "Is that your wife?"

"No, it's not," he quietly replied. "I'm not married, but if I were, she's the kind of woman I'd like her to be in thirty years' time. Let's say she kind of looks after things for me at home. Hopefully, if you don't get bored with me, you'll get to meet her later and have a proper cup of her tea."

"Looking forward to that," she said. "I don't know the meaning of the word boredom, especially with someone like you."

*Better not get too familiar*, he thought, knowing what the main purpose was in getting to know this special person who had been thoroughly checked, vetted, screened and identified to him only a month earlier. This was going to be harder than he thought, fighting off his animal instincts, not wanting to scare her off. He had to get the right balance in his approach to stem any form of personal relationship.

"There he is, in our eleven o'clock position, that's Ben Nevis," he said, pointing towards the snow-covered mountain only slightly masked by a few friendly clouds. "It's not much of a mountain on the scale of things, but it's the best we have here in the British Isles."

"It's big enough for me. I don't like mountains and snow. I'm happy with my standing stones, thank you," she said.

I.P. pondered, remembering a passage he had read in her dossier where it referred to her parents being killed in a skiing accident when she was only a child. *No wonder she's not keen on snow and mountains,* he thought. I.P. had loved the snow-covered slopes in his younger days when he did a bit of ski instructing for a couple of seasons in Geilo until that tragic day when he was detailed to carry out an off-piste search and rescue mission after the avalanche.

"Overhead Prestwick," he pointed out. The Sleeping Warrior or The Isle of Arran on the right, then dead ahead to Ailsa Craig. "Now there's a real standing stone," he said.

"Yes," Mia replied. "I know a lot about that magnificent rock, but it's entirely natural that I am aware of, unless you are going to tell me otherwise."

"No, no," he replied. "We've got nothing on that one."

"And who might the 'we' be?" she asked.

"I will explain later if you allow me to, but let's get down and have some breakfast at my favourite restaurant. You're bound to be starving because I know I am." On that, he pressed the radio transmit button on the yoke. "Good morning, Carlisle tower. Mike Whiskey One," he called.

"Good morning, Mike Whiskey One, you are identified 30 miles North West of Gretna. Report field in sight, left base for 07. More than 10K, zero six five seven knots. QFE 1013."

"Roger, that's copied. Can you ask Ethel to dig out my private stash of tea bags and put the kettle on?" was I.P.'s response.

"Wilco, copied and understood," came the reply with a faint chuckle.

"That was very pally," Mia said. "It appears that you are very well known around airports. Is that another friend of yours?"

Mia was wondering who this man really was. He was certainly not just a casual acquaintance she met at a bar in the wilds of Wannie with a common interest in historic archaeology. *I'm enjoying myself so far so I'm going along for the ride for now*, she thought while conjuring up a pet name for him in her mind. This she usually did for the few people she allowed in her life as acquaintances.

I.P. radioed again. "Mike Whiskey One left base for 07 field in sight."

"Report final number one, cleared to land," came the reply. I.P. skilfully touched down and taxied the Beech Baron to the parking bay nearest to the foot of the control tower stopped and closed down the engines one by one when two very clean cut looking ground engineers dressed in freshly laundered RAF boiler suits chocked the wheels.

As soon as I.P. unlatched the door, a voice said, "Good morning, sir, we've got it from here."

"Thanks guys," said I.P. as he turned to Mia. "There you are, safe and sound. Let's go and see Ethel."

Mia turned and smiled for the first time in this man's company. They each grabbed their small back packs and Mia followed as they walked the fifty metres to the cluster of whitewashed airport buildings and entered the café.

"Here you are. This is my favourite place to eat, especially at this time of day," he said as he directed Mia to one of the yellow, Formica-topped tables next to the window that had uninhibited views of the runway and the mountains of the Lake District beyond.

"This will do for me," Mia said. "And I will have the same as you as long as it's not vegetarian."

"Morning, Ethel," I.P. said as the motherly lady that looked like an Ethel came to the opposite side of the counter.

"Good morning, Mr Penfold. You haven't been away very long this time," she answered. "Tea is on its way. Will it be the usual for breakfast?"

"Yes, please, for two. Thank you, Ethel. And yes, only two days this time, but very enjoyable, I have to say," he said.

A large, rusty, brown earthenware, steaming teapot along with two large, white builders' mugs and a small jug of milk clinked onto the table. "No sugar, Mia?" he asked as he poured the black brew over the milk, turning it a deep, burnt sienna colour in the mugs. They both lifted and sipped the tea with eyelids closed as if they had not had a one for weeks. "Ah, lovely," he said as the two huge soft breakfast buttered bread rolls stuffed with sizzled Cumberland sausage, two thick rashers of crispy rind on bacon topped with an easy over yellow ochre free range egg arrived. They both guzzled away and never said a word until they were finished.

"I was ready for that," Mia said. "Delicious," she said as she turned to Ethel and gestured with her hand, forming a circle with her thumb and finger.

I.P. said, "If you're ready, Mia, let's go for a drive and get you settled into your hotel for this evening. But first since we will be passing, we'll call by Castlerigg as promised." On that, they thanked Ethel once again and walked out into car park. "This is mine," he said and pointed to a gleaming 1965 metallic powder blue 3.8 Jaguar MK 2 with knock-on spoke wheels.

"Suppose this belongs to the government as well…Commander Bond," she replied, smiling.

I.P. laughed loudly and quietly said, "No, it was my father's car." He pressed the chrome button on the handle and the door clicked open for her. A heady masculine scent of wood, leather and a hint of oil wafted into her face from inside, nothing like the smell of cars today, unless it's a Bentley. Mia slid onto the cherry red, leather front seat of the

Jaguar, and he closed the door with that reassuring perfectly engineered clunk. The 3.8 litre vee six fired into life and the Jaguar purred out of the airfield confines with a deep rasp from the only slightly baffled twin exhaust pipes. In thirty minutes, they arrived at the public car park for the stone circle of Castlerigg, thought to be the oldest known man-made structure in the British Isles. "It's only a very short walk from here," I.P. said as they stepped out into the magnificent scenery dominated by the fell known as Skiddaw Little Man in this part of the English Lake District.

"OK," Mia replied. "I'll need my bag." They walked towards the stones and Mia's aquamarine blue eyes lit up like a child on Christmas morning as she stopped and stared at them while taking deep deliberate nasal breaths sending her into a trance like state for a moment or two. "We know very little for certain about why this and many similar structures were built," she said. "More particularly, how or why the sites were chosen, but I have my own theory. I am already feeling the vibes, are you?"

"I do feel inside that these are special places if that's what you call a vibe," he replied.

"That will do for now," she said. "Here, let me try something," she said as she took out a large, somewhat battered, chrome stopwatch from a pocket in her shoulder bag. "I will stand here if you go and stand in the centre of the stone circle. When I give you the signal by dropping my arm from above my head, start the stopwatch on that fancy Breitling of yours and wait. I will do the same and after two minutes or so, I want you to walk back to me and only then we will simultaneously stop the watches on my command." I.P. was intrigued and followed Mia's instructions precisely. After the prescribed two minutes, he walked back to Mia. "Okay," she said. "When I say 'now' we will stop the watches." They both pressed the stop button at the same time as near as makes no difference. "Right, Commander Bond, tell me what time has elapsed."

"Three minutes, seventeen seconds."

On that, she turned her watch and showed it to him. It read three minutes, twenty-one seconds. "That's a full four seconds more than mine, and even allowing for error, it's an incredible difference and suggests time in the centre of that stone circle is running slower than outside it."

"Yes, although that experiment was not an exact science, I believe it is quite compelling, and on a quiet day," she said.

"Quiet day?" he said.

"Yes, it is also my belief that under certain conditions unknown to us there is an infinitesimal non-gravity or non-magnetic energy force and is why these sites were chosen by people in those ancient times," she answered.

"Non-gravity or magnetic, you say?" I.P. enquired.

"There is no evidence for these forces but a lot to suggest it's something else. What that 'something else' is, no one knows. We can only hope that we witness the scientific proof one day," she said, looking up into the sky. "From here, what do you see?"

"A very clear, blue sky," he replied.

"Follow me back into the centre," she said as she took hold of his hand. "OK, look straight up from here and tell me what you see."

"Unless it's an illusion, the sky has a very faint pink-purple haze to it," he replied.

"I agree. It sure does. I've noticed this at Stenness in the crystal-clear air up there but I never mentioned it before," she said. There were a thousand things I.P. wanted to ask but now wasn't the time as they headed towards Keswick. They slowly turned down a winding single lane gravelled road leading into the courtyard of a very beautiful house set back and elevated from the shore of Lake Derwentwater where a couple of dinghies could be seen sailing by. *Very English and very lovely*, Mia thought as the black, glossed, solid, oak front door opened. A red-headed woman smiled affectionately as she walked towards the car.

"Good afternoon, Isaac. This must be Miss Gaustaad," she said.

"Yes, this is Mia. Mia, this is Greta, my Aunt Greta," I.P. replied.

"Lovely to meet you, Mia, come with me and I'll show you around and get you settled in. I hope Isaac is looking after you and not boring you to death. My home is in the annex on the side, but I use the house and invite the ladies around when Isaac is away on business and that's quite often these days. I've no idea what he does, only that he is a civil servant of some kind. This is your room. Make yourself at home and feel free just to wander around. I'll see you later, my dear girl." Greta pecked her on the cheek. This reminded her of her gran that she'd not seen for nearly a year. She felt comfortable, very comfortable and safe in Blue Stones. This gorgeous house by the lake was not old fashioned but did have a subtle art deco theme. Isaac Penfold was a man of fine style. Mia turned the mixer tap lever handle on the freestanding roll top bath and set it for very hot. She picked up the matte green Zippo lighter, struck the flint wheel and lit the two large squat white lily of the valley scented candles and filled her lungs through her nose that naturally lifted and pointed her firm breasts. Mia almost floated in the silky hot water and stayed there just long enough so that her fingers did not start to get prune-y. She towelled her perfectly formed body and took the tiny, black dress that she had hung in front of the radiator after being rolled up in her small backpack for most of the day. The dress was only just loose enough to slip over her head, covering down to her mid thighs. There was no hint of underwear, after all, she had been travelling light. Mia left her room and wandered barefoot, quietly exploring the house and its contents, particularly the artwork. For the first time in a long time, she felt at ease, knowing this was a happy place together with its inhabitants. When she entered I.P.'s study through the open door, he was on his phone saying his goodbyes to Charles.

He couldn't help staring at her for a moment, mesmerised by her natural beauty. "Hello, Mia. I hope you are comfortable; I am glad you came down just now. Can we have a little talk? We can sit here," he said and walked over to the two, pale blue, tartan fabric covered, McIntosh winged armchairs, positioned either side of the bay window with an uninterrupted view across lake Derwentwater.

"Of course," Mia replied, and as if prearranged, Greta arrived with the trolley transporting her fabulous tea and some Jammy Dodgers on a tea plate.

"I've got some things to do so I'll leave you both to talk," she said, leaving.

"Thank you, Greta. You are spoiling me," Mia said.

"Looks to me like you could do with a bit of spoiling," Greta answered, winking at her while closing the door.

"Mia, I must be honest and totally up front with you and have to tell you that I work on behalf of the UK Government by leading a team of very unique people drawn from many different backgrounds and abilities. The one thing they have in common is that they are exceptionally talented in their own ways. They and I are charged with investigating things that cannot be easily explained in the natural world and usually not allowed in the public domain, largely for national security reasons and the good of society everywhere, in the opinion of our leaders. I think you might be surprised by the number of so-called supernatural things that occur on this planet. There is hardly a day goes by when some spooky thing or other does not pass my desk. Believe me, we are kept very busy. You have been identified to me as someone who could make a very valuable contribution to us and consequently to your own homeland. I am asking if you would join us. No contracts, no time limits. It's more than just a job if you want it. Please, at least think about it," I.P. ended.

"I must say I do not feel as comfortable as I did two minutes ago. Sounds all a bit serious, not to mention the fact that I've been stalked in a manner of speaking for goodness how long. Here's me thinking I'd been abducted for romantic reasons, which is more than a slight disappointment," she said.

"I'm very sorry if I've given you that impression. It was never intended that way, but I had to at first get to know you somehow. It's a nice feeling to be flattered by you but I'm old enough to be your father," said I.P.

"Not quite, not in my eyes, Commander Bond," she replied. "Can I think it over?"

"Yes, by all means, please do. You can stay here if you like for a while. In fact, as long as you like. Greta will keep you company if I'm not around. I don't have any appointments for the next thirty-six hours, just a couple of reports to do, but I can do that from here," I.P. replied.

"Yes, that would be good if I can as I'd like to go back to Castlerigg to have a closer look for myself," Mia said. They sat there and drank tea with their own thoughts, not wanting to complicate things, not wanting to force the issue either way. There would be time enough for questions later, maybe tomorrow.

"Hope you don't mind; I thought the three of us could have a Deliveroo evening. There's a Thai takeaway in Keswick and it is extremely good. Don't want Greta to be cooking and fussing over me too much. She is my family, unless you prefer to dine out," I.P. said.

"What? And leave this place? It's much too nice, I could not think of anything better," Mia replied.

"That's enough business for today. Come on, let's go for a stroll down to the shore," he said. While passing through the entrance hall, he reached up and took one of his quilted body warmer gilets, placed it around her shoulders and said, "It's a little bit chilly to be dressed like you are." He couldn't help but notice her raised nipples through her thin, cotton, black dress.

The last of the white sailed yachts headed for the pier in the near distance as she linked the crook of I.P.'s arm to steady herself as she began to wobble on the pebble shore. "This is a magical place," she said. "Have you lived here long?"

"Most of my life. It was my parents' home. They loved it here as I do," he said. "But sadly, they are no longer with us.

Mother died much too young and Father never got over it and is why Aunt Greta came to stay while I was at Cambridge. I think she loves it and it's her home as much as mine now."

"That's very sweet," she said.

"Let's get back and phone for dinner. Don't like to eat too late, if you don't mind. You can choose the wine for all of us," he replied with a wide smile, showing his naturally aligned, white teeth.

"I take it we're having seafood, so for me anyway it should be Sauvignon Blanc or Chablis," she said while browsing through the bottles in the tall, glass-fronted wine cooler, thinking about the king crab legs she loved back home with her gran.

"That should be dinner," said I.P. as the blackbird song door chime sounded.

"I'll sort it out if you stick a few more logs on the fire. We'll eat in here. It's cosier and I can get to know Isaac's new lady friend a little more," Greta said, not knowing that officially, Mia was there on business. Together they all talked, ate, drank the crisp, cool Chablis and laughed a lot around the bright burning pine log fire. The conversation never got deep or serious with Dire Straits 'brothers in arms' playing in the background. I.P. loved their music, having met a member of the band while working on a farm in the north east in his school days where he lived with his parents before moving to the Lake District. He too had the same crush on the farmer's daughter, although much too young for her at the time.

"Feeling a little tired now, so I think I'll leave you two to finish the rest of the wine. Good night and sleep well," Greta said, pursing her lips, blowing kisses as she left the room with a slight stumble.

It was after midnight when Mia and I.P. went upstairs to their separate bedrooms after endless conversation. They were never stuck for things to talk about, such was their growing affinity towards each other. Both had not wanted the evening to end as they said goodnight and closed their bedroom doors behind them. I.P. lay awake troubled that he was having intimate thoughts about this beautiful woman, thinking she was only a girl to a forty-four-year-old man, very much ripe for the picking to any man half his age. He had never felt this way before about other woman in any of his previous relationships, selfishly he knew they had only served his natural lust. Surely, he could not be tempted to surrender to this desire in him that may backfire very badly if he tried to make more of it. Besides, he had already lured her here under false pretences. He also harboured another secret that he had not told her about.

Mia lay awake, aching for this man she hardly knew only yards away across the landing who she had only met forty-eight hours ago. She slipped on the white silk robe, monogrammed with the initials JP, that was hanging beside her dress. Bare footed, she lightly crossed the landing and opened the door to I.P.'s bedroom. I.P. heard the click of the latch and became very aroused realising this beautiful creature was coming to him. Mia stepped, ballet-like, over to his bed and untied the robe. It slithered down her back onto the floor as she stealthily slid leopard-like, goose pimple naked under the duvet beside him. He felt the shape of her large, hard nipples on his chest, then the silky soft skin of the inside of her thigh as she gently wrapped it over him and firmly took his erect penis in her hand. She whispered, "Hello again, Commander Bond. Since you're going to be my boss in the morning, I thought there would never be another opportunity."

He turned and gently but tightly held her close and kissed her open, plump, cool lips. "It's only Friday and you don't start work until Monday," he whispered. She straddled over this horse of a man and finished him off, capturing his sperm being pumped deep inside her. She had never been fucked before, at least not like this.

When Mia came into the kitchen, she was glowing, wearing figure-hugging, stone-washed, torn denims with an equally tight white cashmere sweater. Obviously naked underneath, she was not a tease just the epitome of youth, health and vigour that stirred I.P. "Good morning, Captain Bond," she said in a deep husky voice.

He laughed and replied, "I see you've promoted me."

"For now," she said as she walked up to him and kissed his cheek. "Let's see how it goes on Monday."

He laughed again and said, "Greta is a bit worse for wear this morning. I think one glass of Chablis too many, so she's having a lie in. I've already looked in and given her some coffee. I'll pour some tea for us and make some breakfast, it's not going to be an Ethel special this time, I'm afraid." He chopped up some prunes, dried apricots, dates and a banana and mixed them up with porridge oats, semi-skimmed milk and a glug of carnation milk and set the microwave for four minutes. "This should do us," he said.

"Thought I'd go back to Castlerigg with you this morning before the day trippers, I was fascinated with your little tricks yesterday."

"Excellent idea. Yes, there is something I want to check out," she replied.

I.P. opened the heavy, solid, hardwood garage door to reveal an old, battered green, short wheelbase, canvas topped, fifties Land Rover.

"Was this your fathers as well?" Mia asked.

"No, my mother's," he replied.

"Must have been some gal," Mia said.

I.P. replied, "She certainly was. You can drive, Mia."

I.P. knew she could and was no stranger to this type of vehicle during her time in the Orkneys. She placed her backpack into the centre seat beside the huge gear levers and jumped behind the wheel. Mia was no slouch when it came to driving and drove them straight to Castlerigg without once asking directions. "I'll have to think of a name for you now," I.P. said, grinning.

It was calm and bright as they stood in the centre of the standing stones. They had got there early, thanks to Mia's driving, before the inevitable stream of visitors. Mia took out the laser measuring device from her backpack and started to sight the red laser dot on the north, south and east, west stones and shuffled around in tiny steps in the middle of the stone circle. "This should be near enough to the centre," she said. "Now, Captain Bond, I want you to take this bag out of the circle, find a nice, clean stone or a large pebble, and pop it in the bag. With this, I want you to weigh it," she said as she hooked some digital suitcase scales to the metal strap ring on the bag. "I will not move from this spot. Record its weight in kilogrammes to the nearest two decimal places and come back to me here."

She watched him place a large smooth pebble into her bag and holding it out from his body only. By the scales, he mentally noted the reading of 6.48 kgs and walked back to her. "Why the large pebble?" he asked.

"Bag wasn't heavy enough on its own, what was the reading?" she asked.

"6.48 kgs," he said.

"Okay, weigh it now please." I.P. repeated the process and stared at the reading. "Well, tell me," she said.

"6.36 kgs," he replied, leaving his mouth open.

"Not an exact science, but it does indicate that the energy force here in the centre is not gravity," she said in her own business-like tone. I.P. did not dismiss her comment only to say that they would hang on to the large pebble if she didn't mind.

"Anything else you would like to do or see, Professor Jones?" I.P. enquired.

"Oh yes," she replied, not entirely amused, knowing who he was comparing her to. She unfolded a photocopied layout plan of the circle, with each stone numbered anti-clockwise, starting with the stone, marking the point of the summer solstice. Using her smartphone's compass app, she quickly identified the stone and started to inspect it closely. She knelt down and pulled the grass away near the base to reveal a much eroded but deliberately tooled groove on its edge. Systematically, she inspected each stone and noted the position of very similar grooves on three more of the standing stones.

# Chapter 6
# That Irretrievable Terror

Chief cabin attendant Pam Cairns was on the flight deck, delivering coffee for Jeff and Steve. Jeff had just handed over control to Steve to fly the next two-hour sector that would take them over the UK beyond the Hebrides out over the Atlantic to Rockall. Jeff had his feet on the anti DVT rails, reading an English newspaper, chatting to Pamela.

"Things okay back in club class?" he asked.

"Yes, everyone's nice and settled, all fed and watered for now," she replied.

"Any trouble with Ronnie and Reggie?" asked Jeff.

Pamela laughed and said, "Ah, you mean our two, little, friendly Pugs."

"Yes," he said. "I have to make it my business to know about any special cargo on board."

"A bit yappy on take-off. Their snoring is disturbing the snooty couple sitting behind in row nine. Other than that, they are fine it seems," she replied.

"Well," he said. "Only another six hours so let's keep our fingers crossed."

Leaving the flight deck, Pam said, "Just ding if you need anything."

"Sure will. Thank you, Pam," Jeff replied. Steve had not acknowledged her as he appeared too busy twiddling with things, not that there was much to do other than manage the cabin temperatures and listen out on the radio.

He pressed his transmit button and said, "Good day, Scottish Information. Fire-crest four two six on handover from London, twenty miles south east November Echo Whiskey, heading two seven five, flight level three five zero."

"Good day, Fire-crest four two six Scottish strength five, we have no conflicting traffic. Continue flight level 350 on present heading. Report Tango Romeo November."

"Wilco, report Tango Romeo November, Fire-crest four two six." That was them for another thirty minutes until overhead the Turnbery VOR. He thought as he scanned the glass cockpit screens to confirm heading, speed and height as directed to comply with those latest ATC clearances.

Fred seated in row seven, right-hand window seat had finished his in-flight style German cheese, ham and egg broetchen roll, feeling relaxed sipping his coffee, knowing he was heading home after an uneventful overnight outward journey. Fred worked for the airline as a senior airframe engineer and was, as part of company policy, travelling with the aircraft on its first trip after such a major overhaul in an advisory capacity should it be necessary but not as flight crew. A twenty hour round trip with only two hours on the ground when he would be expected to carry out extensive external checks and liaise with the both outbound and inbound flight deck and cabin crews, but he did have extra legroom seats for both journeys. A little light relief for him after two weeks of pressure to get this leviathan back in the air to start earning its keep. The airline could do with it after very lean times following the Covid-19 lockdown that lasted nearly three months. Fred looked out of his window and watched the calm grey blue sea passing underneath on this lovely day. He knew the North Sea as he had spent ten years offshore, three weeks on and two weeks off in his younger days when he worked on the oil and gas rigs as a helideck landing officer and general go to man for anything mechanical, being already a qualified aeroengine fitter. The money was good then and a lot of American guys were employed because of their expertise in extracting oil. He knew exactly where he was as the coastline of North East England came into view in the distance ahead.

"Hello, Mr Cairns," Pam said, having just emerged from the flight deck.

Fred looked up and said, "Hi Pamela, things okay up front with Jeff and Steve?"

"Mighty fine," she replied. "Jeff's got his feet up and Steve's fixated doing his stuff, flying this big baby."

"Don't tell him I told you but she's doing it all herself," he said, laughing quietly.

"You're only jealous because that was your dream at his age," she said, flicking a napkin gently on the top of her husband's head. "Want anything? I'm on a ten-minute break so I'll sit here with you for a little while."

"No, I'm fine other than my back. It's killing me. Apart from stretching my legs in Frankfurt for half an hour, I've done ten hours in this seat. I've got some deep relief gel in my cabin bag," he said.

"Sorry, my man, but can't be seen going into the toilet with you, otherwise I would have rubbed it on for you," she said laughing.

"Maybe you can give me one of your massages, Mrs Cairns, when we get back home," he replied with a cheeky smile and raised eyebrows. Pam and Fred had been together for twenty years on both their second marriages after meeting at a company 'in pursuit of excellence' training course hosted by Tom Peters. It was very fashionable, gee-up stuff, in the nineties. These guys must have made a fortune during that time but the dot com gold rush and the financial crash put paid to all of that workplace ideology.

"Never mind, not long now," she said, secretly taking her shoes off and flexing her toes under the empty seat in front. "Be glad to get these off for a few days when we get home."

Fred looked her in the eyes and said in a serious tone, "Pam, why don't we just pack up, cash in our chips and head for the hills? We're nearly sixty and we've both had enough, and I think we can easily get by. We'll see a hell of a lot more of the boys and you will not have to stay away for two nights a week. I hate it."

"Yes, Fred, I've been thinking about it a lot lately. Besides, the altitude is making my crow's feet bigger every day. I will miss everybody very much, though."

"You will have to decide sooner or later so why not now?" Fred asked.

"Yes, yes, yes! Let's go for it. I've got some leave so that will do for notice in lieu, this will be our last flight," she said leaning over to kiss him, not caring who was watching.

Jeff felt the slight tremble of the aircraft and automatically looked forward as he knew that they were nearing the UK coastline at Tynemouth, thinking there may be some clear air turbulence because of the Westerly airflow over the Cheviot Hills. The route was very familiar to him and he also knew that in ten minutes, they would fly overhead Keilder Forest, where there would be a lot of thermals on a warm day like this. He reached up and deliberately switched on the cabin seatbelt signs, turned to Steve, and said, "Reduce speed by fifty knots." Steve wound off fifty knots on the airspeed automatic pilot speed bug and the two throttle levers slowly moved towards them with the trim wheel clicking back simultaneously as if an invisible man was piloting while the engines wound down a few percent.

"Just my luck," Pam said as she heard the ping of the seat belt sign. "I've only just sat down. Better go and get our paying guests to sit down. Don't want any bumps and bruises," she said as she shuffled her feet around for her shoes. Fred always travelled with his seat belt loosely fastened and reactively pulled the loose end through the buckle with one hand.

"Okay," he said, disappointedly. "See you later. Take it easy. Love you, Pam."

The tremble gradually worsened, and Jeff put his paper down and took his feet off the anti-DVT foot rails sat up straight and readjusted his seat and tightened his harness. Then the shaking developed into moderate turbulence induced shuddering of the aircraft. "This is unusual," Jeff said. "What the hell is that ahead? Bring the speed down another twenty," he instructed Steve.

"Looks like a purple-coloured cloud. Never seen that before," Steve replied. Fire-crest 426 began to pitch up and down violently as the whooping of the stall warning sounded. Suddenly, the air turned pink inside the flight deck.

"What the fuck?" Jeff shouted as he quickly disengaged the autopilot and fire walled the throttle levers.

"Jeff, Jeff!" Steve shouted. "Everything's closing down on the panel!" he shouted as the screens flickered and went black. "Fuck, fuck! Number one's gone, and fuckin' hell, number two's shutting down."

"Go straight to one two one decimal five and mayday!" Jeff bellowed. *Not that this would help them other than to assist the search and rescue teams to locate the black boxes along with the bits and pieces that were left of them to fill the black plastic body bags sooner than later*, he thought.

There were gasps and screams along the whole length of the cabin as the Boeing was straining every rivet during the severe jolts. It was as if it was being butted by a sperm whale when the oxygen masks dropped above every seat. Most of the passengers were seasoned flyers and, although terrified, they instinctively struggled to place the masks around their nose and mouth some forgot about the gentle tug necessary to open the valve that starts the flow of oxygen.

"Shit, look Jeff, we've got no air speed and the altimeter is whizzing down to zero!" Steve screamed. "We're going to die, Jeff! I'm pissing myself!" he shouted as he felt his hot urine welling around his crotch.

"Put your mask on and hold it together. I need you. She's settling down a bit; let's see what we've got. According to the altimeter, we should have hit the ground by now and I can't feel any Gs, so we are still flying, I think. Don't worry, Steve, I'm shit scared too. It's a bloody bomb or something," Jeff shouted back. Just then, the aircraft went still, very still and although not floating, everyone felt very light. An eerie calm enveloped everyone, thinking that the plane had recovered as they peered through the pink vapour in the cabin.

After fitting her oxygen mask, Mary Larssen snapped shut the Perspex covers on Teddy and Arthur's travel pods and pulled the toggles until she heard the gentle hiss of their oxygen supplies. They did not make a sound as they cowered. She would rather die than let any harm come to those little boys. Hands shaking, she reached for her smartphone and managed to double thumb a message. It was to Mia and the text read:

*On flight NA426. Something terrible is happening. All purple. LYA, Gran.*

She pressed send, doubting Mia would ever see it.

Fred frantically looked up and down the aisle for Pam and saw and heard her a few rows away, instructing, checking and helping the passengers with their oxygen masks. As expected, her training ensured that she had fitted her own portable supply first. His gut was wrenching because he couldn't do anything much other than not to get in the way. If he had put himself in jeopardy by taking his mask off, he had to do something as he knew this plane was in critical danger.

*We've got absolutely nothing. If I had a god, then I would start praying for us all*, Jeff thought as he struggled to find a crumb of comfort for what to do next as there was nothing in the manual or his vast reserves of experience for the situation they were in.

"Okay, Steve," he said, reasonably calmly. "Have we got any power anywhere? What flying controls do we have? What can we try and start? Can we see the ground? I'll hang onto the controls and see what we have if you try and get something going. Anything. An engine would be good or even some instruments. Recycle everything you can."

"All I can see out there is the pinky-purply stuff. Don't even know if we are moving. It's so calm. We must have flown into some kind of vacuum. God, please help us," Steve shouted through his mask with that irretrievable terror in his voice.

"Just get going! We've got about fifteen minutes!" Jeff bellowed. That was the amount of time they had before the oxygen ran out. A lot less if Fire-crest 426 plummeted out of the sky, causing the airframe to overstress and break up in mid-air into a thousand pieces.

# Chapter 7
# Toft Hill

Long before Mia's two-truck convoy arrived, even before the dawn sunrise appeared over the horizon at St Mary's Lighthouse, a 200-metre square plot had been marked out with orange chevroned barrier tape with repeating white lettering, reading, 'Danger. Gas works. Do not cross'. The access points for the public right of way that surrounded Toft Hill were taped off and notices saying, 'Danger. Footpath closed' were nailed to the gate posts.

Mia walked to the red and white ranging pole, already in place, marking the grid reference. One degree, forty-two seconds west, fifty-five degrees, zero two seconds north, in the centre of the clearly-defined plot. She scanned the uninterrupted views of the horizon in every direction. The Cheviot Hills to the north and particularly due east where the sun was rising barely twenty-four hours after summer solstice, Turning to the west using a compass app, she sighted a vector of 240 degrees being the reciprocal of the radial 060 degrees. She had calculated by lining up the grooves, she discovered on the solstice stone and stone number twelve at Castlerigg, suggesting that those people from 3000 years ago already knew the whereabouts of these portals as she put it, convincing her that the other alignments on stones 18, 24 and 32 would lead to three more locations not yet identified in the UK or beyond in the Faroes. They might lead even further as the alignment on stone number 18 directly pointed to the north pole. Possibly, the locations of countless more portals she would never be able to trace unless today Toft Hill gave up its secrets.

Within thirty minutes, the two operators of the lithium-battery-powered GRS carts began a walking pace ground survey, following a meticulous north south square grid pattern. Mia returned to the truck and set up her laptop to receive the digital survey information directly via satellite. She watched her screen for anything unusual or anything at all because if this drew a blank, she had very little else to go on and she would have to abandon her theory and hand over to the ghostbusters' team. The scan width on the GRS carts was only 1.2 metres, so it was going to be a slow process and would take several anxious hours.

"Hazel, quick, come and see this!"

A breaking news bulletin was interrupting The Chase quiz programme on the telly, announcing that Flight NA426 with 295 passengers and crew on board travelling from Frankfurt is overdue at Milwaukee, presumed missing over the Atlantic. Coming close to hyperventilating, knowing that I was party to the real truth, I told Hazel there were a couple of workmen in a gas company van at the end of our cul-de-sac nailing a notice on the gate, leading onto the lonnen, and that I'll go and have a look at what it says as soon as they've gone.

"No need," Hazel said. "It' s all over my Instagram page. Apparently, there has been a gas leak somewhere near Toft

Hill. They've got it cordoned off and there's a heck of a lot of gasmen wandering about, taking readings or something."

"Oh yeah? I thought there was a gas main over there. I saw it being laid about twenty years ago. Maybe it is just coincidence; I started to plan how I could have a snoop then remembered something I hadn't mentioned," I said to Hazel. "You know, yesterday, when I was watching that plane at about the same time, I heard a deep rumble of thunder and the ground trembled. I knew it wasn't thunder, as there wasn't a cloud in sight, so I put it down to blasting at the stone quarry in Matfen, fifteen miles away. You know, when the wind is in the right direction you often hear it. Trouble is that the quarry closed about three months ago. I'd forgotten about that. You know, the quarry where Jonny Thompson worked as a loader driver. The one who wanted to pull that scam to win a mountain bike at Matfen Village fete by guessing the weight of that massive boulder he had in his tractor bucket? He told me the exact weight and we were going to split the value of the prize. I'm pleased the raffle was cancelled due to the rain when no one turned up to buy a ticket, otherwise, we could have ended up in jail. I'm not going to call that Charles guy. He scares me a bit, not a great fan of the establishment. It will be easier to get an audience with the Pope, and it's probably nothing anyway."

"That's what you said the last time. I've got this Mia Gaustaad's card. I will call her for you and tell her what you've remembered, not that bit about the bike though," Hazel said, tutting as she replied.

"Very interesting," Mia replied over the phone to Hazel. "I may, if you don't mind, call in and see you both alone this time as I'm working in your area on behalf of the gas company. I'll call you, I've got your numbers. Goodbye, and thanks again, Hazel."

Two hours had gone by and Mia's computer screen was ever so slowly starting to fill up from the north boundary of the grid, with only minor radar hits. It kept showing, in black, some random rocks and boulders. Then suddenly, she saw a straight black line scaling about one metre. On the next trace, the line thickened. Then, again and again, after each sweep, the black image kept on getting wider, showing definite square edges. Mia picked up her phone and pressed a quick dial button and started to speak. "Hello I.P."

I.P. answered, "Hello, Mia, that's a bit formal. What happened to the Bond bit? Have I been demoted already?"

"Afraid so," she said. "That happened the day I set foot on Delta Five One Zero."

"So disappointed," he said. "I was beginning to get attached to it. You got anything out there?"

"Could be, looks promising," she said. "But it'll be another couple of hours or so. Too early to be certain right now."

"That's good news as there's nothing much coming from the 'Ghostbuster' or 'Little green men' teams yet, although the 'Terrestrial' lot have said that there was some noticeable seismic activity exactly where you are standing, yesterday around midday. Obviously, I know that it's unlikely that a mini earthquake would bring down an airliner from 35000 feet, but it may have some relevance. Listen, Mia, you do whatever you think is necessary. I need to go, I've got a COBR meeting with the cabinet in a minute or two."

"Okay, Commander Bond. I may need someone to do a lot of digging very soon. I'll get back to you. When will you be free?" she asked.

"Send me the images as soon as you think you have something, and I will get back," I.P. replied.

The black images on her screen grew larger every few minutes, she thought these square geometric shapes were unlikely to be natural so surely this must be a man-made structure of some significance. The digital survey information kept coming, and soon she realised that this was some form of circular construction and from her anticipated projection of the curve, it would be at least 100 metres in diameter with a circumference more than anything similar she had ever come across. Mia saved the image she had so far and e-mailed the file to I.P. After a further two hours, the ground radar surveillance mapping had revealed about a quarter of the now apparent circular structure, clearly showing some very large, very regular square cut rectangular megaliths. The major difference was that they appeared to be lying flat, spreading away from the centre like the petals of a huge sunflower, and the readings indicated that these stones so far were about 600 millimetres below the surface at their nearest point. Mia thought to herself, *Got to start exposing these stones.* Rightly thinking, it was going to be a massive job.

"Hi, Mia," I.P. said as she answered. "Sorry, I couldn't get back earlier. Looks like you've really got something up there. Charles has seen it and insisted that we show it to the PM and the cabinet, so you can imagine the level of questioning going on that we simply cannot answer. They have already put a danger area around Toft Hill and a NOTAM has been issued with immediate effect. You couldn't fly a kite in there without it being shot down. I wish you could have been here. They were impressed with your little experiments at Castlerigg. Bottom line is that they want the site opened up as soon as possible to see if we can throw any light on this Abora Effect."

"Those little experiments were hardly scientific proof of anything, yet just followed a hunch. I'm going to need a lot of bodies with a bit of knowhow up here," she replied.

"Okay, Mia. I was impressed with those things too. Bit like water divining. Hard to believe but also difficult to dispel. I will arrange all the help you need. I've already spoken to the Bods at English Heritage," I.P. said.

"Aren't you going to give the game away, though? Because it's going to require about fifty guys with their caravans, VW campers, mini diggers and all sorts of other paraphernalia. Not to mention that these gnarly but nice people will descend on the village pubs at seven o'clock every evening," she said.

"Well, so be it. With the exception of Will and Hazel Surtees, there are no other people in the public domain that know what exactly is going on. As far as anyone else is concerned, this is just another archaeological dig brought about by the discovery of some Beaker People artefacts during the routine maintenance of a gas pipeline. And listen to me, Mia. You will be in charge out there by order of the highest authority in the country. We are not having some hairy-arsed, balding men with ponytails taking over who think they know better to boost their own egos. Mark my words, they will be mobilised by tomorrow together with few of our own operatives mingling around with hand trowels who are to report to you along with everyone else, are you clear with that?"

"Perfectly. Captain Bond, over and out," she said.

*Mmm been promoted again. What that was for*? he wondered.

By the following morning, the radar surveillance data was complete. It was astonishingly well detailed and unambiguous with every megalithic stone petal of this gigantic sunflower shaped structure shown clearly. There were seventy-nine of them. The printout also indicated that the entire area in centre could very well be paved.


Hazel knocked at the front window and waved for me to come out into the garden. "Hey, look at this," she said and pointed towards the gate leading onto the lonnen.

*Christ*, I thought. "Is the garden shed locked? Lock up your daughters; the gypsies are here!" I said as I watched a convoy of beat up old Land rovers pulling caravans, whacky minibuses, converted ambulances and hauling trailers noisily passed the end of our street, heading up the muddy track towards Toft Hill.

"You better pop your eyes back in and close your jaw. Mia Gaustaad just phoned to ask if we were at home," Hazel finished telling me.

I watched Mia Garstaad get out of a white and orange, gas company four by four, dressed in a green boiler suit and matching hard hat.

"Hello, again. How are you both?" she said. "So glad you could meet me at such short notice."

I told her that we were well, considering we could have been the only people to witness the loss of 295 poor souls onboard that aircraft.

"Yes, it's desperately sad, but you never know. There's a massive search going on right now. There might be survivors," Mia said. "If you're wondering why I'm dressed this way, I can tell you that I am really an archaeologist seconded to the UK Government. Isaac Penfold is my boss and there is something of a lot of interest to me I am investigating over at Toft Hill."

I told her that I thought she was Charles Stanley's PA she did not answer but gave me a bit of a death stare.

"Can you tell me about the earth tremors and this thundering noise you heard?"

"All well and good, but they are searching in the wrong place for that aircraft, aren't they?" I questioned.

Mia moved quickly off that subject and asked me to describe in more detail the noises and tremors. "Did it seem to come from the Earth upwards or from the sky, towards the ground, for instance?" I told her while I couldn't be certain, it seemed to me as if the tremor preceded the double boom of thunder and suggested to me it was very much the latter, very like the sonic booms when an aircraft is breaking the sound barrier that I've heard once before.

"Very good," she said. "That does make a difference to me."

"Would you mind a look up there sometime?" I asked her.

"Don't see why not. I will invite you as my expert guest but you'll have to wear one of these outfits as officially it's off limits, but for you guys, I'll arrange your clearance. The motley crew you see going up there are from English Heritage and are just the muscle right now. I'll contact you when there's something for you to see in a day or two. As always, keep it under your hat. You wouldn't want Charlie boy after you again, would you?" she said, smiling.

*What a lovely girl*, I thought. *Pity she's a yank.* I doubted I was an expert at anything other than being an old git as Hazel continuously reminds me.

Mia instructed the workforce to start with a two-metre wide trench, running roughly east west to pick up the solstice stone, clearly the largest trace result calculated at approximately 1.7 metres wide by 5.8 metres long. Normally, a dig of this magnitude would take years but Mia needed to expose this structure quickly. Already, the weight differential experiment was the biggest at about twenty percent, proving to her that there was an unknown anti-gravity force at play. Expanding on her theory, she thought these guys might start floating in a minute or be blown to kingdom come, but who knows, ignorance was a blessing at that time.

"Got something, Miss Gaustaad!" someone shouted. "Look! I think it's a floor," he said as a powerfully built woman gently scraped at the clay to reveal more of a highly polished black stone, perfectly cut in a hexagonal shape about 300mm across.

"Looks like Hematite," she said, truly astonished by this find. Six more of her colleagues swooped into the trench and started scraping as if they had gold fever. This was better than gold, given that these stones were worked by human hands some 3000 years ago. Stone after stone of this beautiful back paving slabs expertly butted together were now being revealed.

I answered my phone.

"Hi, Will. Mia here. I'm up on Toft Hill, got something you deserve to see. I'll bring you some gear in about twenty minutes."

"Okay, I'll be ready," I told her.

It was day three after the incident. Looking into the excavations, I was gobsmacked at what was being unearthed. A large area of polished, black cobbles reflected the sunshine as if they had been laid yesterday. It was a hive of activity within the curtilage of the huge site. I thought I recognised a few faces here and there, but I must be surely mistaken as most of the guys were the spit of Phil, the dig of the Time Team, and the women looked much like an eighty's newsreel clip from Greenham Common. Over on the eastern edge of the compound, there was a tented area with a couple of burley types, seemingly guarding the entrance flap.

"Follow me, Will," Mia said. "As they say in the movies, you ain't seen nothing yet."

The two burley guys stood to one side and lifted the flap for us. The LED lighting inside the large Gulf war army tent powered by a gently fluffing generator was intense. Mia peeled back the tarpaulin and said, "We've just finished cleaning it."

I could not believe my eyes. There was a huge, obviously expertly tooled by stone masons, piece of polished pink Peterhead Granite. I knew this as I used to be a building surveyor in a former life. It was at least twenty feet long, about five feet wide and at least eighteen inches thick, lying perfectly level. About six feet from the top was an inlaid circular piece of solid gold, about fifteen inches in diameter, unmistakably an effigy of the sun. Below this also inlaid an equally impressive, life-sized bronze effigy of a winged man, so beautiful that Mr Gormley may have swallowed his tongue with the sight of it. The whole thing was magnificent, very much a Rolls Royce version of Stone Henge. Mia began to tell me that it was fairly obvious that these stones would have originally stood upright, but for some inexplicable reason they were purposely laid flat so that they could be covered over and lost forever, it seems. I asked her if she could estimate how long ago would it have been built.

Mia replied, saying, "It's certainly no crop circle, that's for sure and there's no record of it as far back as human history has been documented so it must several millennia old. It could eclipse anything that has ever been discovered by mankind."

Just then, Mia's text message alert sounded. As she read the text, she turned as white as a ghost. Tears began to well in her eyes then stream down her cheeks. She was just about to faint when I.P. arrived inside the tent and gently took her in his arms and said, "Yes, I know. I'm so sorry. It's your gran, isn't it? She was on Fire-crest 426."

Mia went limp and sobbed, saying, "How, how I've only just received this right now? It's her message to me from three days ago."

"Would you like to come back to mine to see Hazel? I think it's better if you can get away from this for now," I said.

"Yes, Will, I would like that very much," she replied in a little voice.

"I will look after this for now," I.P. said quietly. "You can come back when you are ready. Thank you, Will, that's very, very kind of you."

I.P. had just read the passenger manifest for flight number NA 426 and immediately recognised the name Mrs M. Larssen. He already knew Mary Larssen but did not have the courage to tell Mia how.

Hazel gave Mia a massive hug and kissed her on the top of her head. "I'll make you a nice cup of tea. Sit there and try to be calm. They are still searching, you know. We would like you to stay here for a while. We don't want you to be alone in that hotel. Besides, I'm sure you'll want to go back to Toft Hill sooner than you believe at the moment and its only yards from here," said Hazel.

# Chapter 8
# The Impossible Descent

Dolla Dingaman is a loner but not a sad man. This was not his registered name he would use for a passport, not that he would ever want one, it was a name given to him by one of his street friends. He was christened Billie Bob Smith by his parents, way back when soul-crushing political correctness was not even heard of. He had chosen a life of solitude with the exception of a mangy, three-legged mongrel that he named Long John. He had befriended him in this place he knew as his home, in the middle of nowhere to westernised mortals at least thirty miles away from the nearest human with no contact to the outside world, other than his CB radio in this empty, stifling, dry as a bone, red desert of a land. It was in the far distance, barely visible, as if a mirage was Uluru in his people's sacred temple.

In a former life, Dolla worked the Cockle Bay Wharf, at Darling Harbour, Sydney, Australia. This was his pitch. He used to mesmerise the thousands of tourists hopping on and off the ferries with the unique rhythmic pulses of his didgeridoo. It was a musical instrument he had been taught to make out of a eucalyptus tree trunk, hollowed out by termites. He would do it while wearing only a chamois loin cloth, enhanced only by the stark white body paint on the blackest of black skin. This tall, slim, Aboriginal Australian was never short of a buck or two as the hand-outs mostly in Australian paper dollars hardly stopped floating into the cardboard box placed at the noise end of the dingy. There was also the selfie contributions after each three-minute rendition that came very natural to him once quickly into his trance like state. There were also his unframed canvas paintings, at least two dozen at any one time neatly piled by the side of his feet, guarded by Dinga, a scrawny half-bred dingo with a ball sack the size of a grapefruit. His traditional paintings readily sold for twenty dollars apiece, cheap considering the artistic merit that every single skilful dot of paint added to the many hundreds and sometimes thousands more to create a unique artwork that told dream stories that never aged. Over the thirty years he had plied his trade and entertained millions of visitors to these parts, he had managed to bring in a small fortune. He never married but equally had never been short of intimate female company, having a mysterious attraction that Caucasian men could hardly compete with. Naturally, these fleeting encounters with mostly infatuated white girls never lasted. By the age of fifty, he had more than enough money to buy his own humble place that resembled a house that came with literally miles of land, impossible land for others but not to Dolla Dingaman.

"Jeff, Jeff," Pam shouted as hard as she could through her mask while banging on the flight deck door with the side of her fist. "You alright in there? What's happening? Please, please answer!"

"Yes, we're okay, I think," came the muffled sound of Jeff's voice through the lock fast door. "We cannot let you in here, is it terrorists?" he shouted.

"No, no, but its frantic back here," Pam screamed back.

"Pam, listen to me, is Fred okay?" said Jeff.

"Yes, he's the only one calm," replied Pam.

"Can you get him up here fast?" Jeff bellowed back through his mask.

Jeff heard the heavy thumps on the flight deck door. Fred shouted, "Jeff, it's me, Fred."

Jeff shouted back, "I'll let you in as soon as you convince me there isn't one of those murdering bastard slime bags with a blade at your throat."

"Definitely not," Fred answered as loud as he could. "You know me. I'd rather die than let one of those fuckers in there."

Jeff reached down and opened a small, concealed flap beside his feet, put his hand in the snug compartment and placed his fingers around the grip of an automatic pistol. Someone had to be trusted with a weapon as a last resort after the horrific events of nine eleven. "Keep trying," he bellowed to Steve who appeared rigid with fear. "I'm going to let Fred in. Take your shoes off and batter the fuck out of anyone who gets past me. He might be able to help us, so we've got no option"

"Okay, Jeff, good luck," Steve replied, almost whimpering.

"Right, Fred, I'm going to open the door. If there is any cunt with you, they are dead," Jeff screamed like a raging bull. While he cocked and raised the gun to face height, he released the lock and pushed the door slowly open with one foot. Both hands' palms forward, Fred stood there hyper venting into

Pam's portable oxygen mask. "Come in, Fred, what's going on back there?" he asked, putting his hand on the big guy's shoulder and lowering the gun.

Fred replied, "I think we've got everybody on the oxygen. There's no sign of any slime bags, and it's definitely not a bomb or decompression. What have you got up here?"

"We've got nothing. She's completely dead. We've tried everything. All we know is we don't seem to be crashing," Jeff replied.

"Christ, what's that smell?" asked Fred.

"It's poor Steve. He pissed himself a few minutes ago. I think it's gone a lot further than that now," Jeff said, rather sadly.

Fred reached over and put his hand on Steve in a reassuringly fatherly way. "You're doing fine, Steve. Let's see what we've got here," said Fred. He scanned the screens, dials and warning systems and said, "Yes, she's dead as a Dodo. You've done everything to try and restore power?" Fred asked.

"Everything," Jeff replied. Fred looked at Jeff with a cold resignation.

As Fire-crest 426 began to tremble once again, Steve shouted, almost croaking, "Jeff, Jeff, I've just seen something outside!"

"What, what is it?" Jeff screamed, fearing the worst.

"It was a patch of blue sky," Steve said, frantically. Jeff and Fred looked forward to see glimpses of blue in the purple hue ahead. Just then, Jeff looked at the flickering pointers on the auxiliary altimeter as they started to revolve slowly. Clockwise at first, then they started to whiz around in a blur. The needle on the analogue air speed indicator began to rise.

These back up instruments didn't require to be electrically powered, they only relied on dynamic and static air pressure to drive them. Fire-crest 426 began to pitch and bank violently and Jeff instinctively grabbed the yoke. "She's smoothing out. Look the sky's clearing. Can't see the ground!" Jeff shouted.

"No, because we're inverted!" Fred shouted back.

*Christ all fucking mighty*, Jeff thought. "We still have some manual stabilator and an inboard aileron control on each wing, but it's going to be a fucking monumental job for you boys to haul her the right way up."

"We've got the airspeed. It's 320 knots! And look, the bloody altimeter says 38700 feet!" Fred exclaimed. "Steve, I want you to swap places with Fred. I need muscle. I want you to call out the speed and altitude every fifteen seconds. I'll tell Fred when to pull and push. Let's get her the right way up and slowed a bit if we can. We need to get her down to fifteen thousand so we can breathe. I think we have about five minutes' oxygen left. Not nearly enough, but we must try. There's only one place that this two-hundred-tonne glider is going, and that's back to terra firma, one way or the other. Right, Fred, we're going to bank to the left and keep her going over to about 90 degrees. I'll have to guess until I get a horizon of some sort."

"345 knots, 37600 feet," Steve shouted through his mask.

"Fred, when I say, 'pull back', I mean give it all you have. If we overspeed, we'll break up. Pull, pull now!" Jeff bellowed. "I've got the ground, keep pulling."

"395 knots, 35400 feet," came another frantic loud call out from Steve.

"Okay, Fred, turn to the right now to level the wings. Keep pulling back, for fuck's sake, I can't hold her myself."

The veins in Fred's neck were just about bursting as he turned and hauled back the yoke.

"360 knots, 34000 feet," screamed Steve.

"Keep the nose coming up. Come on, Fred, help me, I need some more. Let's try and get her down to 250." The sound of the rush of air howling over the windscreen began to subside. "Okay, I think we've got her."

"285 knots, 31000 feet!" Steve gasped in the background.

"She's going to be a heavy twat to get down in one piece," said Jeff as he started to lose what remained of his captain's cool, calm etiquette.

"265 knots, 28000 feet," came another of Steve's loud panicky calls.

"Okay, we'll keep her steady at that. Let's have a look and see what we've got," said Jeff.

"If that's the ground, it looks very red," Fred announced.

"I don't care what colour it is. Let's keep her going. We'll worry about that when we're down to 15 thousand and we can breathe, then have a look," Jeff answered.

"250 knots, 24000 feet," Steve called out through his ever-tightening throat.

"Look! Look over there," Fred shouted. "Punch me in the face and tell me this is not a nightmare!"

"What is it?" Jeff shouted.

"It's fucking Ayres Rock! It's unmistakable! It fucking is," said Fred.

Jeff looked in amazement. Sure enough, about eighty miles away, no doubt it was Uluru. "Look, Steve, over there, 11 o' clock," Jeff said, pointing.

"You're bloody right. No mistaking that. 245 knots, 18000 feet," Steve said, almost gagging, with a mouth as dry as a witch's tit.

"Bugger me gently is this an episode from the Twilight Zone," Jeff exclaimed not even wanting to try and fathom how they got here.

Now that Fire-crest 426 was the right way up and slowed to 260 knots, descending at about 1500 feet per minute. She was a marginally less of a strain to handle, provided they did not let her have her head. *Easier said than done*, Jeff thought.

"250 knots, 14000 feet," came the robotic call from Steve in a slightly calmer tone as he started to regain his wits.

They were now able to breathe. 295 people and two dogs began to gasp in lungful of air in the now gin-clear cabin.

"It's just like a flat, red desert from here," Fred said.

"It could be like the Rocky Mountains from up here, for all we know. We'll not find out until we've only got about five-hundred feet to go and that's when the fun starts. Glad I watched Scully five times," said Jeff.

Pam staggered through the cockpit door. "They're all still strapped in from fifteen minutes ago when you put the seat belt signs on," she said, almost normally.

"Crash positions, crash positions now, right now. We've got no engines and barely any control. We'll do our best for them," Jeff called out, loud and clear.

"Okay, Steve, Fred, here's the plan. No promises, but it's our only chance. Steve, keep the call-outs coming, it's gonna be vital to me when we get down to 500 feet. Fred, now listen up carefully. We've got no flaps, no leading-edge slats and no undercarriage and there's a lot of drag from those dead engines. She's not going to create enough lift at less than 200 knots with clean wings, so she'll stall below that and we are history. We'll keep her going down at 220, at fifty feet. You got that, Steve? I said at fifty feet we will flatten her out and hold her off as long as it takes or we can, so we'll be hitting the ground at about 190. We must keep the nose coming up and the wings level even after we hit. It's not possible for me to do it on my own. I will tell you when, okay, Fred? Got that? You'll get your wings after this and let's hope it's not angel's wings," Jeff said, taking the deepest breath of his life.

"Jeff," Steve said. "We don't know what the wind is doing and there's no water anywhere to find out. The prevailing wind in these parts is northwest, and look, Uluru is almost on the nose, about fifty miles away. It's north, according to the magnetic compass. Can I suggest you use it to line up with the hazy horizon? It'll help you to keep her straight and level and the land is as flat as anywhere else as far as I can see around here."

"Thanks, Steve, that's a bloody good idea," Jeff replied. "Fred, you got that?"

"240, 7000," Steve called out, regaining a little composure, if you could call it that.

"Okay guys, buckle up and good luck. It's going to be fucking rough," said Jeff while tightening his harness until he hurt.

The cockpit was heating up rapidly to match that of the searing outside temperature and the sweat started to soak their shirts and drip off their chins.

Steve kept the calls coming. 235, 4000... 230, 2500... 230, 1500... 235, 1000...

225, 500...

"Okay, Fred, steady. Pull back, keep going, pull back," said Jeff firmly.

"195!" Steve shouted.

"Ease off a little and hold it. She's slowing too quickly. Hold it there, Fred. Steady, steady. Here it comes. Keep the nose coming up. Come on, baby, come on, baby!" Jeff shouted.

There was a spine crushing dull metallic crunch as Fire-crest 426's two massive engine intakes hit the ground scooping up tons of the red sandy grit and rock in one cavernous gulp reducing the speed by 50 knots in a tenth of a second ripping the engines clean off their pylons to roll head over heels behind them, with this amount of weight and drag instantly jettisoned Fire-crest 426 bounced 30 feet back into the air. "Pull, pull get the nose up!" Jeff screamed. The nose rose, and Fire-crest 426 belly-slapped into the ground, still travelling at 150 knots with grinding thunderous lurches that seemed to go on for an eternity. Contorting like a snake, the screeching airframe eventually came to a standstill, almost intact, but in three parts, separated by gaping tears in the fuselage. Dust clouds everywhere but no fire, Fire-crest 426 lay shrouded in a red dust cloud. There was deathly silence.

The flight deck bulkhead had pushed the control panel and both yokes, back trapping Jeff and Fred. Their legs and feet were mangled inside a ravel of wires and twisted metal. Steve lay motionless, face down behind them, bleeding profusely from a wound on his forehead, but they were all still conscious.

Pam struggled to release her seatbelt but had to change hands because of her wrist that was obviously broken. She looked out of the huge, gaping hole in the side of the aircraft.

Just in front of row seven, where she had sat in Fred's original seat, and in a fleeting semi-conscious moment, thought, *I didn't think England was a red desert*. Pam forced herself out of the seat and started to take in the horrific scene on board Fire-crest 426, there were bleeding gashes and twisted limbs everywhere but strangely not a sound from the passengers as she scrambled along the cabin and did not come across anyone that wasn't at least alive, then suddenly, she thought of Fred and her blood ran cold.

Mary Larssen had clearly broken her left hip as the pain took her breath away when she tried to turn around to see to Teddy and Arthur. They were nowhere to be seen or heard. Next to where they should have been was another wide jagged split down the side of the fuselage, she dreaded the thought of them being catapulted into oblivion, suffering alone and started to quietly sob. To her, they were more than just dogs, they were as good as humans.

# Chapter 9
# The World Heritage Site

"How do you feel this morning, my dear girl?" asked Hazel. "Did you manage to sleep at all?"

"No, I didn't sleep much, if at all. But your bed is very comfy, and I got a lot of rest. I felt so alone and lost, just being here with you and Will made me feel much better than I would have. It was such a shock that I didn't even know she was getting on that plane. My gran, Mary, was the only real family I had left, apart from a few distant cousins in Norway that I've never met. It's such an empty feeling," Mia answered sorrowfully. "The same feeling I had when my parents kissed me goodbye one day and never came home."

"Your gran probably wanted to give you a nice surprise. We don't know what to say, other than Will and I want you to know that you'll always be welcome here," said Hazel.

"Thank you, that's most kind, but I've decided that getting back to work will be best for me until I go back to Muskego to sort out Gran's affairs. There's a lot of people depending on me for some answers to this awful situation," Mia replied.

"Yes, I'm sure that will be best for you," said Hazel. "But don't put yourself under any more pressure."

I heard the noisy, old Land rover pull up in a puff of blue smoke outside and told Hazel and Mia that Mr Penfold was here. I.P. got out and reached in the passenger seat and lifted out two large bunches of flowers and a small box. I.P. came to greet me at the front door.

"Good morning, Will. I've come to see how Mia is, if you don't mind. This is for you," he said as he handed me the box.

"Thank you. Come in," I said. "Mia is in the back with Hazel."

The box contained a bottle of my favourite Vodka. I wonder how he knew that.

I.P. slowly approached Mia, gave her the yellow roses and put his cheek next to hers. She automatically put her arm around his neck and held him very tightly.

"These are for you, Hazel, and thanks for looking after the star of my team, can we have a moment to talk?" I.P. asked.

"Mia," he said. "I have to go to London. Can you tell me what you would like to do about Toft Hill? There's no one I'd rather have on it but you."

"That's good of you to say. I had already decided to go back up there today," Mia replied.

"That's great. I'm getting picked up from here shortly so I'm leaving mum's Land rover for you. It's yours to keep. I know my mother would have wanted you to have it. Besides, you work well together. I think the old girl likes you. If it's not too soon, tell me what you think might be going on up there. It's out in the open, thanks to the flint arrowhead people. That there has been an archaeological find of the century, according to the tabloids, but that's all they know. The matter with the aircraft is still and will be HD for a long, long time."

Mia managed a brief smile and said, "Okay, Commander Bond, I'll keep you posted. And thank you for your mother's jeep. Tell me her name."

"It was Julia," I.P. replied quietly.

"Okay then, Julia can look after me as I will her," Mia said.

"Oh and by the way, I've just taken Karen to the site on Toft Hill, thought it might be a comfort to you. I hope you don't mind," I.P. said.

Karen was one of the original ten M and W's appointed to Mia's team. A palaeontologist, also a solitary girl. Very beautiful with the possible exception of her right eye that shocked most at first glance. Mia's first impression was one of pure admiration; in the shortest of time, she became her first real friend.

Mia arrived back at Toft Hill as the last of the outer stones were being cleaned off by Karen, aided by a bunch of real ale guys with tiny trowels and sable-haired paint brushes. There was nothing like this structure on Earth, at least in such pristine condition. It could have been constructed yesterday, but it had been 3000 years since the last human being had clapped eyes on it.

Mia did not have conclusive proof, but she knew this was a 'Grand Portal' with mysterious but fantastic forces that could transport these ancient people's secedes or human sacrifices into paradise or oblivion towards their Sun God. She deduced that when these victims of sacrifice or even volunteer martyrs did not produce any worthwhile benefits or the people got tired of this barbaric suppression and rebelled, they laid flat the stones and buried them out of sight and harm's way forever. The problem now was that today, they

95

could not do the same because sure as hell the site would be plundered. It would have to be designated a world heritage site so that that it and the population could be protected. She also knew that it would have to be closed to all living things around the 20$^{th}$ June every year, the time of the summer solstice.

On day five, since Fire-crest 426 went missing, Mia's e-mailed report to I.P read:

*It is my belief that the Toft Hill stone circle is a ritual building with similar origins to that of Stone Henge, Castlerigg, Stenness and most certainly many more structures lying undiscovered in both the world's hemispheres, particularly north and south of the latitudes, known as the tropics of Cancer and Capricorn. It is not the actual structure that is of real consequence other than the fact that, to carve out and move seventy-five eleven-tonne granite megaliths from as far away as Aberdeen by presumably human beings three thousand years ago is beyond modern day comprehension. It is the reason why the location for such sites was chosen in the first place. This being that since the creation of Earth, billions of years ago, when it contained natural forces from the creation of the universe, the origin and substance of which is unknown to us other than the so-called big bang as it is definitely not gravity, magnetism, radiation, dark matter or even God particles. This is why I believe it is the force of Mother Earth itself. It is apparent to me that this force can stay relatively dormant for millennia and is barely detectable other than to some people who are usually dismissed as cranks, witches and the like, who have a certain craft. It is a fact that two aircrafts were transported into possibly another dimension at the exact same point and height over the Earth at the exact same minute of the year when the sun is at its highest, it is, however, pure coincidence that these aircrafts were in the wrong place at the wrong time. This Mother nature force is not evil to mankind; it is her natural protection mechanism to fend off the sun's rays to protect the poles and maintain a temperature equilibrium. Earth does this by accelerating these particles to more than the speed of light, creating a force field at the edge of the atmosphere visible to us by the action of the sun's photons being dissolved, causing them to turn into a magenta haze. As humans, we do not have the ability to prove this force's existence, neither do we know if there is life after death, but there is an abundance of evidence if we choose to believe it.*

Mia's iPad had hardly had the chance to register the e-mail as sent when her Facetime alert rang and read 'Commander Bond'.

"Hello, Mia," I.P. started to talk. "I've just seen your e-mail. I, for one, believe you, and Charles is pretty convinced too. If you've read some of the files we have on out-of-body experiences and visits to the next world, life after death is definitely a foregone conclusion. There is a cabinet full of them locked out of sight in my office that should not see the light of day, so your theory is enough for me. Besides, I've got some very important information to tell you about if you promise not to think too far ahead and raise your hopes."

"Okay, I.P., what is it then, tell me?" she replied, briskly.

"The wreckage of an airliner has been located and the first indications are it is that of Fire-crest 426. There are survivors, but details are very sketchy. Here's the thing – are you sitting down? It's in the middle of the outback, about twenty miles from Uluru, in Australia."

Mia's knees weakened and she didn't say a word.

"Listen, Mia, there's no time to waste. There's a VC10 leaving Brize Norton in less than an hour with a team on board including Charles. Believe it or not, he's having it stop off at Newcastle to pick you up. He's insisting you come to Australia. We'll meet you south side EGNT in two hours. We'll be on the ground for 10 minutes max."

Mia froze and never got time to answer before her screen went blank.

# Chapter 10
# The Saviours and Survivors

Dolla Dingaman never heard the whoosh of Fire-crest 426 as it passed over his roof at no more than 300 feet. He wasn't awake, not because it was early nor was it that there wasn't much to get out of bed for other than to have his fourth piss of the night, nor was to feed Long John or to get to Uluru for his once-a-week stint as a tour guide – it was more to do with the bottle of Captain Morgan's rum he had consumed neat only six hours ago. He hadn't even felt the earth tremors or heard the thunderous crashing noises, they had just melded into his delirious dreams. He was awakened by Long John's tongue slobbering around his nose and mouth.

"For fuck's sake, can a man not sleep around here?" he grunted and spat while pushing the dog off the bed. Long John wobbled to the door and started whimpering while trying to scratch it open, precariously balancing on the one back leg he had. "Okay, okay old boy," Dolla said. "You got prostate trouble as well." Dolla opened the door and was greeted by four, googly, dark brown eyes looking longingly up at him. "Christ, where the hell have you come from?" he said, staring at the two little black dogs covered in red dust. "Suppose you guys better come in. Looks like you could do with a drink."

The two, little, black pugs demolished a jug full of water that Dolla poured into Long John's large, stainless steel bowl. Then they ran back to the door and barked in stereo while trying to scratch it open.

Dolla knew that they hadn't come far as they were still wearing their body harnesses with name tags. "Arthur and Teddy, eh? Come on, let's go and see who you've ran away from," he said, thinking he would see a Winnebago with its greenhorn outbackers just being nosey.

Teddy and Arthur swaggered to the end of the veranda in that 'I think I'm a big dog' pug fashion and started to yelp in the same direction. Dolla looked and couldn't believe his eyes. Three hundred yards away, he saw the sun's mirrored reflection on the huge tail fin of an airliner. "Bugger me gently," he said under his breath, still wearing only his underpants, and as fast as he could manage, he threw a large, heavy crowbar, some rope and a hand axe into the trailer hitched onto a motortrike parked as he had left if butting up to the veranda. This Heath Robinson machine was knocked together from a 1200cc Harley Davidson that he had built from parts he had salvaged from Barney's scrap yard 30 miles away on the nearest paved road where many tourist vehicles were taken having given up the ghost and been abandoned except for the snakes and spiders. Dolla fired up the Harley that sounded like two, unhappy, alpha male tigers. He told Long John to stay put and roared off almost naked in a cloud of red dust with his frizzy, long, greying hair flowing behind, towards the wreckage fearing in his gut what he was going to find.

Dolla arrived at the crash scene and was astonished by the size of the thing. He had never been this close to an airliner before. The flying doctor's Piper Navajo but not this. There were three passengers sitting quietly outside the aircraft and he could see several more starting to slowly emerge out of the doors and jagged gaping tears in the fuselage. Dolla thought to himself, *At least they can move, so they are probably okay for now.* He circled the trike around the entire plane and checked for any signs of fire. Luckily, there was none other than the pools of kerosene dripping out of the wings, so he decided he would access the flight deck section first as it looked as if it had taken the brunt of the impact. Dolla unhooked the CB handset, clicked the transmit button and started to make a call.

"Dingaman to Metal Mickey, come in please." He repeated, adding, "This is an emergency."

The CB crackled and a voice said, "Morning, Dolla, what's up?"

Dolla replied, "Barney, now listen up. There's about a hundred tons of alloy in my backyard. It's in the shape of the biggest aeroplane you've ever seen. Trouble is, it's got a lot of people still inside and some of them are hurt bad."

"Christ, Dolla, have you been on the Captain's Jamaican fire water again?" Barney answered.

"Barney, I'll suck your dick if it's not true," said Dolla.

"Okay, Dolla, that won't be necessary. I'll make the calls. I believe ya, thousands wouldn't," said Barney.

Dolla took the crowbar and axe, then squeezed into the cabin just behind the cockpit and pushed and pulled his way forward into the crumpled space where Jeff and Fred sat trapped in their seats. Steve was already trying desperately to free them, blood dripping off his chin.

Dolla said quietly, "Okay, fella, I've got it from here. I'll get them out, go and try to stop that bleeding."

Dolla leant forward and said, "Good morning, captain. Can't remember giving you permission to land in my backyard. Don't struggle, I'll get you both out of here." He started to lever the panel away from their legs, asking if they were hurt. It was obvious that they were, but he needed to find out how badly.

Jeff looked at this very black and almost naked man and replied, "Glad to see you, my friend. Yes, it's my knees. They're smashed up a bit, but apart from that, I'm okay. Just get this off and please pull me out. Got to see how my passengers are but see to Fred first."

"No, no," Fred said. "I'll be okay once this bloody thing is lifted off my legs. It's only that my ankle looks like my foot is pointing the wrong way."

"Okay, fellas, one at a time. It's gonna hurt real bad, but it's either this, or I cut your legs off," Dolla said as he gestured with the axe. "Gotta level with you guys. Help is at least two hours away and you are creating your own lake of fuel around you. Did you manage to make a mayday?" Dolla replied, trying to lighten the mood.

Jeff replied, "No, all our systems went down about thirty minutes ago over England."

"Fuckin' hell, captain, sure you didn't bump ya bonce? This is bloody Ozzie, man! England's 10,000 miles away in the direction you're pointing!" exclaimed Dolla. "Oh and by the way, I've got a couple of your passengers back at my place by the names of Teddy and Arthur, just as well they woke me up."

"What's your name, my friend?" asked Jeff.

"Billie Bob Smith, but people around here call me Dolla," was the reply.

"Cheers, Dolla, you've saved a lot of lives here," said Jeff.

"No mate, I think you and your two buddies up here have done all the lifesaving," replied Dolla as he heaved and pushed the crowbar but could barely shift the panel crushing their legs. "Listen guys, I'm gonna have to try something else but it's risky. If I don't get that pressure off your legs you both gonna lose them and that's at best. If you both hold this bar in position, I will tie a rope to it and pull it with my motor through that opening where the window was. If this thing moves then you are gonna have to haul yourselves clear with this other rope behind you, just scream your fuckin' heads off when you're out. Can't risk running the motor too long in case the fuel goes up." *Just as well they had left the white-hot heat of the engine parts behind*, he thought, not knowing that they had stopped and cooled off well before they ploughed into the ground.

Dolla set up his motor trike with the rope through the window. He gently took up the slack then started to gun the Harley while watching a pool of Kerosene growing closer, he then heard Jeff and Fred's screaming and shouting and hoped against hope that they were free.

Two hundred and ninety-five souls came out of the wreckage into the open one way or the other. Most crawled out, the rest were dragged. Most were injured but all were alive when the first helicopter arrived overhead, followed by the sight of a big dust cloud and flashing lights on the horizon.

"Hello, my dear, dear Mia," Mary said, lying in the bed as Mia appeared in the doorway of the hospital sideward. Mia burst out crying uncontrollably as she hugged her gran as if she never wanted to let go.

"How are you, Gran?" Mia asked.

"Oh just a little bit stiff but I think I'll live. I'm sure I will be fine when these screws in my hip settle down. Come here, let's have a look at you. A little dark under the eyes, other than that you look well, in fact very well indeed considering what you must have been through. My dear girl, you are pregnant, aren't you?" Mary Larssen said to her granddaughter.

Mia never answered and wasn't even shocked at the question. She said, "I've brought you some visitors; we've managed to sneak them past the nurses outside." I.P. stepped into view carrying Teddy and Arthur, their little piggy tails wagged frenziedly.

Mary looked up at I.P. and said, "Thank you, Isaac, it's nice to see you again."

"You know each other?" asked Mia looking in astonishment backwards and forwards at each of them in turn.

"Yes, we do," said Mary Larssen. "Isaac pulled Karolina and Jakob, your mother and father, out of the snow after the avalanche. He stayed for more than an hour trying to revive them before help arrived."

# Chapter 11
# Life Goes On

Captain Jeff Clark didn't mind limping around the golf courses with Lada these days. He had got his handicap down to an admirable seventeen in that short time that was very good going considering the permanent injuries to his knees. They laughed together almost nonstop with Lada's profanities that almost got them drummed out of the golf club on several occasions. He had long since refused to give interviews after agreeing a deal with the airline, their insurers and the FAA to corroborate the story that Fire-crest 426 had lost all systems and power when it flew into a hypersonic jet stream that carried it around the world for nearly four days, he could never account for the fact that their ordeal only lasted thirty minutes as far as he was concerned.

First Officer Steve Baumgartner never re-joined the company and disappeared the following winter working as a reclusive ice road trucker in Alaska. Steve very quickly became very older and wiser and never sought the limelight. He was last recorded to be the commander of a float plane water bomber in California. The danger and extreme flying did not faze him in the slightest; his fear was only enough to keep him focused. He never wasted a bomb run and was praised by his counterparts fighting the horrendous wildfires on the ground.

No one ever got to know the part Chief Engineer Fred Cairns played on the flight deck that day, but Jeff did anonymously send him a pair of pilot's gold braid wings that he proudly sports on his Avionex leather flying jacket. If ever anyone earned them, he did.

After the months of interrogation and enquiry, Pam and Fred went into self-imposed exile, tending a few rare breed saddleback pigs along with six named pet chickens, a goat, a dog and two cats on their smallholding on the shores of lake Michigan. They both looked and were a lot healthier than ever before during their working days, screaming across the skies in that artificial world. Most importantly, they were now very happy people who did not dwell on the flashbacks or neither did they stay in hotels anymore. They focused on only their future together on the ground and without knowing it, never leaving each other's side.

As for the rest of the two hundred and ninety-five, who knows they all had their own ways of dealing with what they remembered. Precious little in most cases because of the mild hypoxia during that insane thirty minutes or was it four days.


I.P. sat in his study, listening to the birds through the open window at Bluestones on this lovely, English summer day.

"Daddy, daddy," came the sound of a high-pitched voice as the little, blonde girl ran up beside him.

"What is it, Mary, my little darling?" he said, lifting her up. "Come here. I love you so much, I could eat you."

He laughed, nibbling at her tiny ear.

"Stop it, stop it, daddy! Your whiskers are too jaggy. Mammy and Auntie Greta are baking my birthday cake in the kitchen and mammy says she can't reach the taps because of little commander bond in her tummy. It's my little brother, you know."

"How do you know it's a brother?" I.P. asked her, smiling.

"I've seen him on the picture, and he's got his thumb in his mouth and I felt him kick me," said little Mary.


Billie Bob Smith stepped out of the gigantic red Boeing 747 belonging to Australia's flagship airline at Heathrow, London. He took a deep breath of the crisp, cool, fresh English morning air. He had never smelled air like this before. *It was beautiful*, he thought. This particular airliner was the most distinctive in the fleet and probably the world with its unique livery copied directly from Dolla Dingaman's pointillist paintings that sold for heck of a lot more than twenty dollars apiece in those years on the harbour front in Sydney as a result of becoming a somewhat reluctant celebrity following that fateful day, five years earlier. Dolla had spent the past couple of years rebuilding his house on exactly the same site and installed sweet clear running water filtered and pumped from the aquifer on his land. He now had electricity generated from an acre of solar panels, and of course the internet. He kept his old Harley motor trike to stand as a gate guardian. His new transport, a mighty four by four Ford Ranger XLT Ute, specially adapted with an electric ramp for his dear old mate, Long John, to wobble up into the cab beside him. The red yute was of course fitted with a CB radio and a huge aerial, although he didn't expect to be calling for help anytime soon. Apart from the billion to one chance of an airliner crashlanding on his land, the real life changer for Dolla was meeting Rosa Jones, a journalistic cultural correspondent for the Blackfella Film Company, who had travelled from Sydney the day the news broke about the heroism of a solitary Australian aborigine to interview him. Dolla's dreams while in his trance like state playing his didgeridoo for all of those years had materialised in front of his eyes.

Little Mary flying around, holding out her cape of her 'superwoman' outfit, heard the crunching of the taxi's tyres as it came up the green-slate, chip driveway at Bluestones. She started to squeal while jumping up and down like Zebidy. "It's Granny Mary! She's got Teddy and Arthur and she's carrying a basket!" Little Mary said, almost gasping.

"Well you better go and help her with it, then," I.P. said. "And mind the steps."

Little Mary ran out to meet her Granny she loved so much and hugged her around her legs with both arms. "What have you got, Granny Mary?" she asked.

"It's your birthday present," Mary said as she gently placed the basket on the ground beside little Mary. "Look, it's Teddy and Arthur's little babies. This little one is yours to keep and look after. Granny is going to keep the biggest one for now."

"But, Granny, I didn't think Arthur was a mammy pug," said little Mary.

"No, Arthur is not a mammy dog, but they are still his babies all the same. We will have to think of a name for this little boy. Come on, let's show Mammy and Daddy," Mary said to her.

"Here's another taxi," Little Mary squealed. "I'll go, I'll go!" she exclaimed as she skipped to open the door.

There stood Dolla, almost blocking out the daylight. "You must be Mary Penfold who is five years old today, so this is my gift to you from the other side of the world," he said as he gave her a beautifully hand-painted, half-size didgeridoo he had made himself. "My name is Billie Bob Smith. I have flown here on a gigantic aeroplane from Australia, just to see you," he said. Little Mary did not say a word. She took the didgeridoo and ran back into the house.

"Mammy!" squealed little Mary. "There's a big, big man with a black face and huge, white teeth. His name is Billie Bob, and he gave me this," Mary said, holding the didgeridoo towards her parents with outstretched arms. "What is it?" Little Mary asked.

Mia replied, "Well then, I think it must be Dolla Dingaman, so you better give him this. It's your present to him. I'm sure he'll tell you all about this didgeridoo he's made himself as his birthday present to you, all the way from home near Uluru, the home of his people known to us as Aborigines. They are a wonderful, kind people who have a history dating back thousands of years," Mia said as she lifted the other little black pug out of the basket and gently placed it into Mary's cradled arms.

Dolla fell to his knees and kissed little Mary on the top of her head, then said, "This must be Dinga then."

"Yes," she replied. "He's yours to keep." She kissed Dolla like an angel on his black cheek.

The doorbell went again. "I'll get it this time," said I.P., jumping out of his seat. "Good morning, Hazel, Will. So pleased you could make it," said I.P. while gesturing them to come in. "How's life in Dinnington?"

"Very different," I replied. "Can't get moved for bus trips. Chinese tourists, people floating around in white smocks chanting mantras and the planes don't fly directly over my house anymore. But never mind, we're too long in the tooth to move now so we'll just have to put up with it like the rest of the village-ites. I have managed to wangle a little job as a tour guide though. I think the bods at English Heritage must have been impressed with my insider knowledge and my building surveying background unless someone around here pulled a few strings." I.P just winked and smiled at me, but never uttered a word in that direction.

Isaac and Mia Penfold decided to let their guests sleep late during the morning after Mary's birthday party, singing, dancing and listening to music accompanied by little Mary's valiant balloon cheeked attempts at blowing her didgeridoo while they prepared breakfast for everyone along the lines of Ethel's special Cumbrian baps given that there wasn't a single vegan under their roof. They were excited that Dolla had invited them all back to Australia for his traditional aboriginal marriage to Rosa, where little Mary could have her face painted as guest of honour carrying her hand painted didgeridoo.

"Mia," said I.P. quietly.

"What is it, Commander Bond?" she replied.

He looked her in the eyes, placed his hands gently on her shoulders and said, "The remains of three sheep have been discovered in a remote Welsh valley. They all have injuries consistent with falling from a great height. The thing is, from their dye marks, they have been identified as belonging to a farmer who grazes them at Castlerigg."